BLOOD SKY

WESTERN STORIES

WILL COOK
EDITED BY
BILL PRONZINI

CENTER POINT LARGE PRINT
THORNDIKE, MAINE

This Center Point Large Print edition
is published in the year 2014 by arrangement with
Golden West Literary Agency

Additional copyright continued on page 271.

The text of this Large Print edition is unabridged.
In other aspects, this book may vary
from the original edition.

Set in 16-point Times New Roman type.

HC ISBN: 978-1-62899-253-3
SC ISBN: 978-1-62899-254-0

Library of Congress Cataloging-in-Publication Data

Cook, Will.
[Short stories. Selections]
 Blood sky : western stories / Will Cook ; edited by Bill Pronzini. —
Center Point Large Print edition.
 pages ; cm
  Summary: "Seven stories centered around conflicts men of the
  West faced with nature, animals, people, and even within themselves"
  —Provided by publisher.
 ISBN 978-1-62899-253-3 (hardcover : alk. paper)
 ISBN 978-1-62899-254-0 (pbk. : alk. paper)
 1. Large type books. I. Pronzini, Bill. II. Cook, Will. Blood sky.
  III. Title.
PS3553.O5547A   2014025808
813'.54—dc23

Printed and bou
by TJ Internatio   Ltd

TABLE OF CONTENTS

FOREWORD

A commonality among writers is the holding of numerous jobs and positions prior to pursuing a literary career. Before Will Cook began writing fiction in 1951, his employment resumé was as long, if not longer, than most. The difference between Cook and other writers, however, is that everything he chose to do to earn a living can be classified as adventurous. He ran away from his Indiana home at sixteen to join the U.S. Cavalry, served as a U.S. Army Air Force pilot during World War II, and after his discharge worked as a bush pilot in Alaska, a logger, a deep-sea diver, and a deputy sheriff in northern California. His hobbies other than flying, with one exception, were equally daring: sports-car racing, sailing, and boat building for a planned year-long cruise to Polynesia. Even the one exception, singing in barbershop quartets, reflects his unconventional approach to life.

The first three short stories to carry his byline were published in March of 1953 in a trio of Popular Publications' leading Western magazines. His first novel, *Frontier Feud*, appeared the following year as a Popular Library paperback original. Until his sudden death from a heart attack in 1964, at age forty-two, he was a fictional workaholic, publishing sixty short stories and novelettes in such magazines as *Dime Western*, *Max Brand's Western Magazine*, *Star Western*, *New Western*, *Adventure*, *Argosy*, and *The Saturday Evening Post*, and fifty novels under his own name and the pseudonyms James Keene, Wade Everett, and Frank Peace. Several other novels appeared posthumously.

The Western genre was Cook's primary interest. All but one of his novels is either a traditional or historical Western. (The lone exception, *We Burn Like Fire*, a contemporary tale with a sports-car racing background, was published by Monarch Books in 1959.) The best of his fiction was several notches above the average fare of the period. One theme about which he wrote particularly well is the clash between Native American tribes and the U.S. Cavalry. "Comanche Captives", a series of related stories first published in serial form in *The Saturday Evening Post* (3/14/59–4/25/59), was filmed by John Ford as *Two Rode Together* (Columbia, 1961). These stories were eventually published in an integrated trilogy: *A Saga of Texas Book One: Until Day Breaks* (Five Star Westerns, 1999), *A Saga of Texas Book Two: Until Shadows Fall* (Five Star Westerns, 2000), and *A Saga of Texas Book Three: Until Darkness Disappears*

(Five Star Westerns, 2001). Other standout novels utilizing similar themes include *The Brass and the Blue* (Random House, 1956) as by James Keene and *Last Command* (Fawcett, 1964).

Notable among his novels with standard Western themes are *Badman's Holiday* (Fawcett Gold Medal, 1958), about a frontier sheriff at odds with townspeople, ranchers, and his own violent nature, and *The Rain Tree* (Five Star Westerns, 1996), which chronicles the lives and rainmaking efforts of settlers on the arid Western plains. Three of his historical Westerns are particularly good: *The Texas Pistol* (Random House, 1955) as by James Keene, a rousing adventure set in the Big Bend country of the Texas Republic in the 1840s; *Sabrina Kane* (Dodd, Mead, 1956), the moving story of a woman in frontier Illinois in 1811; and *The Breakthrough* (Macmillan, 1963), which addresses the hardships and bigotry faced by a returning Native American veteran of the first World War.

Cook's fiction is generally character-driven, rather than plot-driven, and depends largely on conflict for its development—conflict between man and Nature, man and animal, man and his enemies, man and his friends, man and woman, man and himself. In the stories collected here, these various struggles create and maintain suspense, and give his characters depth and the reader insight into their lives and times. "Blood

Sky" from *Western Story* (12/53) deals with the effects of Nature's unpredictability on a small group of ranchers, when a protracted drought followed by an extended period of rain leads to frayed nerves and sudden violence. "The Contest" from *The Fall Roundup* (Random House, 1956) pits a determined hunter against a "bold and magnificent enemy," a vengeful buck he once wounded, in a powerful clash of wills. "The Far-Travelin' Man", published here for the first time, is a fine, off-trail character study of revenge and redemption set in the Tennessee hill country. In "Wildcat on the Prod" from *Star Western* (12/53), a hot-headed young Texas cowboy locks horns with a rival over the woman he loves and learns some hard lessons as a result. "Fight at Renegade Basin" from *3-Book Western* (2/57) concerns a horse trader's battle to keep his homestead ranch from the clutches of an unprincipled land baron, his efforts to solve the mysterious disappearance of $800 in cash, and his encounters with three volatile women.

First and foremost, Will Cook was an entertainer. These seven action-packed and vividly characterized stories demonstrate why his Western fiction earned him an enthusiastic audience during the 1950s and early 1960s.

Bill Pronzini
Petaluma, California

BLOOD SKY

I

At five o'clock in the afternoon the sun hung like a molten gong against the edge of the world and heat was a thickness that made Jim Wilder draw deeply for wind although he had opened three buttons of his faded shirt to await a cooling breeze. Out on the land the grass lay, brown and dead, while away from the ranch yard, where horses hadn't chopped the earth to dust, cracks split the adobe-hard face.

To the east the flatness ended and flat-topped buttes rose, now multi-colored from the palette of the dying sun. The rocky summits threw back a hot breath as if they, too, were against the insignificant men who dared to scratch at their face in the process of their empire building.

Ward Cox sat on his sun-bleached porch and stared at the baked wasteland. Jim Wilder squatted on the bottom step, his long legs tucked under him, his raw-boned face severe with his thoughts. Emmaline Cox sat in the rocker, but her small movement produced no relief and she

11

stopped, plucking at the sweat-damp dress that clung to her arms and full breasts. Ward Cox lifted an *olla* and drank, then spit it out onto the hard earth.

"Damned water's like swill," he said, and his wrinkled face turned hard and stubborn.

Jim Wilder glanced at him, then shifted his eyes to the girl. The tension he felt was close to the surface, but he pushed it down. "Those clouds look promising." He pointed to the northeast.

Cox turned his head slowly, as if he feared a sudden movement in the heat. He stared at the fluffiness, then said: "They was that way last week, too. Cuss my hide iffen it don't just tease a man. It gets your hopes up, then goes away. I'm havin' a devil of a time recollectin' when it did rain last."

"Last year, Papa," Emmaline said tonelessly, and the old man turned his eyes on her quickly, as if she had committed an inexcusable error.

She lowered her glance to her folded hands and lapsed into a long silence. She was a pretty girl with wheat-colored hair, but the land was slowly placing a mark on her. Already her skin was sun-darkened and small lines formed at the edges of her eyes and mouth, making her seem older and more grave than her twenty-three years.

Jim Wilder murmured: "You ought to go into town, Emma. You need company."

"What for?" her father said suddenly. "Ain't

this place good enough for her?" The sharpness of his voice whipped across the porch, a tempered thing near the breaking point, and he took a firm grip on himself because of it. He blew out a long breath and added: "Damn this heat anyhow."

"I got one water hole left," Jim Wilder said, and his brows went into a crooked line of worry because he didn't like to think of it.

"I saw Walt Buchard in town last week," Cox stated. "He's determined to use your water. His is plumb played out."

"Can't begrudge a man water at a time like this," Jim said.

Ward Cox snorted through his nose and Emmaline studied Wilder with a genuine concern. "Buchard's the kind who'd figure that for weakness. Give him a little now and he'll take it all later."

"Not much left he can take," Wilder said, and stood up.

Cox seemed surprised. "You ain't goin'? In this heat?"

"Stayed too long already," Wilder said. "Anyway, I want to stop off at Philmore's place on the way home." He looked toward the horizon and saw that the clouds had grown into high, fluffy mounds with a strong vertical development. "Still looks like rain," he added.

Cox stared at the man, then shook his head sadly as if he had suddenly surrendered all hope.

Wilder was a simple man, worn thin by hard work and trouble. He had a square face with high cheek bones and wide-spaced eyes that looked at a man with an open tolerance.

Cox said: "Damned if I can figure you, Wilder. You been hit bad . . . if not worse than any of us, but I yet got to hear you cuss about it. Don't nothin' bother you?"

The old man had touched on a raw thing and Wilder rolled a smoke to hide it. There was a deep temper in the man and it showed occasionally in his eyes, but habit kept it dormant, habit and a strong will. He said: "I figure that when a man cusses Nature, then he's lost . . . Nature's got him licked. It'll rain. You just wait and see."

"I been waitin'," Cox said and settled into a sullen silence.

Jim glanced at the girl and drew a pale, reserved smile, then walked across the bake-oven heat to the barn to get his horse. Ten minutes later he was cutting across the flat basin toward O.B. Philmore's place at the edge of the breaks. He kept remembering Emmaline's smile. It was as if she deliberately withheld herself from him, and at the same time enticed him in the many small ways so common to women. It had always puzzled him, this deep shyness of hers; he saw no reason for it other than some shadow in her mind.

The sun had died and a grayness settled over the land as he rode into Philmore's yard. There was a small flare of activity near the bunkhouse, as the cook finished the dishes by the cook shack door.

Virginia Philmore sat on the edge of the porch in a pair of thin Levi's and a gray work shirt that hung open against the lingering heat. She buttoned it when he dismounted, but let the tail hang on the outside. He sat beside her and cuffed the hat to the back of his head. She didn't speak and somehow Wilder didn't think it was necessary. She had a tall, well-turned body with dark hair that fell loosely across her shoulders. Her face was dark and a little on the thin side, but there was a full, expressive mouth and eyes that regarded him levelly, with a man's frankness.

O.B. Philmore came out, grunted when he saw Wilder, and sank into his chair to stare out toward the black flatness. Hair lay in wet chunks on Wilder's head when he removed his hat and scrubbed a sleeve across his forehead. "Only a crazy man would be out riding in this heat," O.B. said critically.

"Night's here," Wilder argued. "It'll cool off now."

"Yeah . . . around three in the morning," Philmore complained. "Damn, if we'd only get some rain!"

"I been over to Ward Cox's place," Jim stated. "He's been hit plenty hard, although he hates to admit it."

"He's a damned fool!" Philmore said with

15

considerable heat, then clamped his lips together in a thin, intolerant line. He was a thin-faced man with dark, brooding eyes and a mustache that drooped, giving his face a sad look.

"How's Emmaline?" Virginia asked quickly. It was as if she sensed her father's rising temper and hoped to delay it by switching the topic.

"She's fine," Wilder said, "and I guess a little lonely. Not much company for her there alone."

"I'll ride over if it turns cool," Virginia said. She glanced toward the northeast as bold fingers of heat lightning sent jagged splinters of light earthward to cause a momentary brightness. The cook turned to watch it. Even the men by the bunkhouse halted their talk to stare with hope.

Wilder said: "How's the water holding out for you, O.B.?"

"What water?" he snapped. "I got a small seep that's turning into a mud hole. There's another back in the buttes that's dry as a bone. Walt Buchard was over the night before last asking for the use of my seep, but I told him to go to the devil."

Wilder's eyebrows pulled together thoughtfully. "You and Walt was friends, O.B."

Virginia glanced at her father, but it was too dark to read his face. She went in to light a lamp, coming out a moment later to sit in the pale light streaming from the open door.

O.B. Philmore wiped a hand across his face and

said: "I don't know, Wilder. Times like this a man don't have any friends. Sometimes I think it'd be easier all the way around if I just packed up and let the wind have the place. I lost three hundred head this year . . . more'n I shipped last fall." He paused to pack his pipe and light it. "As I see it . . . you got the plum . . . that place in the hills."

"I'm no better off than you are," Wilder said mildly.

Philmore grunted in disagreement and the bowl of his pipe glowed and died. "Even if it rains, water has to come a long ways before I get any of it in my creeks. You got a couple of basins up there that ought to hold twenty, thirty thousand gallons in two days' hard rain. Makes a man wonder sometimes."

"Makes a man wonder what?" Wilder asked, but only his voice was relaxed. He'd heard that tone in Philmore's voice before—the night they'd hung Howie Rayburn on a cross beam in the barn.

"You're a newcomer," O.B. said. "Five years ain't a long time, Jim. Me 'n' Walt never objected to you settlin' up there at the time, but we could have made another mistake."

"Don't make a mistake and try to move me off," Wilder stated. "I ain't Rayburn, remember that."

Philmore's chair protested as he threw his weight onto the arms, but Virginia rose in a quick, fluid motion and said: "Care for a walk, Jim? We may pick up a breeze." She didn't wait for an answer, just took his arm and led him away from the porch.

They passed the corral and walked beyond it until night swallowed the buildings. The ground was still hot beneath the thin soles of his boots and this slight exertion caused sweat to bead his face and soak his shirt.

She said: "I still like it here . . . even with the heat." Her voice was soft and her talk impersonal, but Wilder sensed the deep call to life that ran beneath the surface. He had felt it the first time he had met her. It kept calling him back time and time again.

"After that statement I don't feel so lonesome," Wilder said, and watched heat lightning flash again. "Your father's getting proddy," he murmured. "And it ain't a good thing. Temper is short enough as is."

"Sometimes a man just has to hit out at something," Virginia said. "You really can't blame it all on the man."

"Can't blame it on the heat, either," he said. "Buchard's gettin' pushy. He wants some of my water. The last time he wanted something a man got hung."

"Why don't you give it to him." She spoke quickly. "It would save trouble."

"I'll give it to him because he needs it," Wilder said. "I don't give a damn about his trouble."

She indicated that they had come far enough

when she swung around and started back. "Tomorrow's Saturday," she said. "There's a dance in town."

It was in her voice, the thing that called to him, strong and clear. It caused a smile to break across the severity of his face. "I'll be there," he told her.

He left her at the porch, said good night to her father, and mounted his horse. He cut south past the barn and rode into the hills, coming out an hour later in a deep valley high above the basin floor.

His two-room cabin sat, dark and forlorn, against the rising land. A small corral and barn stood away from the house; the tool shed and a dried-up well were to his left. Two years ago this land had been grass heavy, and water came sweet and cool from the well. It had belonged to another man then, but now he was dead and spider webs hung across the well combing. No grass poked through the cracked land under his feet. He was down to his last eight steers and even now these roamed wild in the badlands beyond.

Wilder halted suddenly when he realized someone sat on his stoop. Emmaline Cox rose and touched him. He led her into the dark cabin and fumbled around for the lamp. She sat down by his table when soft light flooded the room, causing her to blink against the brightness.

The furniture was hand-made, painstakingly fitted by a man who possessed an infinite patience and a deep conviction of his own self-sufficiency. Emmaline glanced around the room as she had done before, and felt the same sense of defeat. She had hoped for a rumpled bed, or dirty dishes piled high in the sink, or any sign of a man's slovenly habits, but she found nothing and it disturbed her. She needed a weakness for a foothold to his affection, but his actions told her that he had no need for a woman, and she was the kind of a woman who wanted a man to need her—to show that need.

He said: "It's late for you to be out, Emmaline."

She had changed her dress for a man's shirt and light-colored jeans that fit tightly around her curved hips. Her mouth was full, but whatever emotion churned within her was dampened by her shyness and reluctance to reveal herself. She said softly: "Father is proud, Jim . . . but he needs water badly."

"Everybody needs water," Wilder stated, and took the coffee pot to the stove. He kindled a small fire, then sat down and rolled a smoke.

Emmaline clenched her small hand into a fist and massaged it tightly, saying nothing. Wilder glanced at her and, as before, sensed that words were near the surface of her lips, but would never be spoken. It seemed to him that she feared rejection and found that fear stronger than her longing.

The coffee boiled over with a loud *hissing* and

he rose and took it from the stove. She waited until he poured, then murmured: "Sometimes I think you don't feel anything for anybody, Jim. You don't get mad . . . you just don't care. Sometimes I think you just don't see me at all."

He held the cup between his hands, his heavy forearms flat on the table. Lamplight bathed his face with shadows and his stubble stood out, stiff and black, making his face harder than it really was.

"Emma," he said gently, "let's keep it nice and simple between us. Let's not dig into each other's mind and try to think things that were never there in the first place."

He saw a quick hurt cross her face and lowered his eyes. It had been that way between them from the first—he could never relax when he was with her.

"You're going to give Walt Buchard water," she said. "You could give Father some, too. I don't understand you, Jim. You don't like Buchard, not since he and Philmore rode up here after Howie Rayburn, yet you let him use your seep."

He spoke with great patience as if he was trying to convince a small child that the candy was all gone. "What water? If Walt moved twenty-five head over here, they'd drink it dry in two days." He scrubbed a hand over his face for weariness was pressing on him. "Tomorrow I'll take a bath and go to town. That'll be a luxury because next week I won't have enough water to shave with." He slapped the table hard, displaying for the first time the ragged end of his temper. "This country's goin' to hell proper. Your dad and Walt were damned near at war the last time they met. The merchants had closed off credit, tryin' to hang onto what little they have left." He blew out his breath between his teeth, adding: "I wish it'd rain for a solid month."

"I wish things had been different between us," Emmaline said softly.

Wilder's head came up and he said: "How different, Emma? We've laughed together and danced and looked at the moon. What could have been changed?"

"Us," she said simply. "Maybe we should have said a little more to each other . . . but it wasn't that way, so why talk about it."

"That's right," he told her. "Why talk about anything? I think, if I passed out, a person would have to throw a bucket of dust in my face to bring me around."

He rose and went to stand in the open doorway. Heat still lay heavily, a lingering aftermath of a now dead sun.

She brushed past him to leave, then stopped. "I'll see you in town, then?" He nodded, but still she waited. It was an old pattern to Wilder and he reached out to touch her. The desire was in her eyes, but she raised her hands instinctively. "No!

Please," she said, and went after her horse. He waited until the sound of her pony died, then blew out the lamp, and took off his clothes. Once he could have listened to the night sounds, but now there was nothing but a thunderous silence. He had the distinct feeling of being alone in the world. It had been different when Howie Rayburn was alive. The man had laughed a lot and sang crazy songs and, when the moon was right, played cowboy with another man's cattle. But Rayburn was dead and no one missed him but Wilder.

II

There was a faint coolness in the hours that preceded the dawn and Wilder woke and fixed his breakfast. He carried water from the seep a quarter of a mile away, then did his chores before the heat became strong.

Light came early to the land and with it a sun, big and full of blinding heat. It climbed quickly, as if it were eager to scorch the burned waste it had already laid. It was a quarter up when Walt Buchard and a rider came into Wilder's yard.

Buchard was not a tall man, but there was a tremendous width to his shoulders. He had a clean-shaven face, but the jaws still held a blue cast. They were wide jaws, heavy and big-boned, giving the appearance of a man with mumps. He didn't bother to dismount. He pulled his horse close to Wilder's door and stated: "I drove ten head over. I'll see that they don't get in your way."

"Be careful. Not much water left," Wilder said.

"I appreciate what there is," Buchard said. He waved an arm at the rider who waited fifty yards beyond, then turned back to Wilder. "If we get rain, you'll fill up quick."

"O.B. mentioned that last night," Wilder said softly, and watched the heavy man.

Buchard had the habit of toying with his hat thong while turning something over in his mind and now his fingers were busy. He said: "Me and O.B. figured you'd let us water here until the creeks fill up."

"Maybe," Wilder said noncommittally.

Buchard's lips grew heavy and he fingered the latigo thong. "By God, now . . . you want to see us go under?"

"We are under," Wilder stated. "It'll take us ten years to build back up to where we were. Face it, man . . . all we got left is the land we stand on and that's blowing away."

Buchard stopped toying with his hat thong and shifted heavily in the saddle. "Wilder," he said bluntly, "I don't like you. I never liked you since we strung up Rayburn."

"There was never any love lost," Jim admitted, and watched a brazen temper wash into Buchard's face.

"You never make a mistake, do you?" Buchard said. "All right . . . you made your stand, now I'll make mine. When your basins fill up, by God I'll drive to 'em and you better not try to stop me."

"Don't let your temper get away from you," Jim cautioned, and waited for Buchard to take up the stick. It was out in the open now where both of them could see it, but Wilder felt no relief because of it. Some curtain of caution came down in the heavy man's mind, for he wheeled his horse and joined his rider at the seep.

Buchard would like to have driven his cattle into the sink, muddying it up, but his need for water was stronger than his temper and they held them at the edge. His first impulse of the morning was to gather his whole herd. It would have meant a fight, but he was remembering a slim man who held a rifle that night and fought to save Howie Rayburn. It would have given him pleasure to stampede them through the sink—he was in that mood.

Wilder came up a few minutes later on a horse, and Buchard saw that he had belted a revolver high on his hip. He sat quietly, saying nothing while Buchard and his rider made the gather and drove them back. There was no thanks in Buchard and Wilder found that he didn't give a damn.

He rode into town early; the sun still beat down slantingly against his back. At another time he would have felt a twinge of guilt at this outward display of his laziness, but now he had reached the end of his rope and didn't care about that, either.

Warpaint sweltered in the heat. The clapboard siding on the buildings was cracked; the planks of the boardwalk curled into corrugated roughness. There was little traffic on the street although a few horses dotted the hitch racks. Wilder turned into the stable at the end of the street and stripped off the saddle.

Howard Manafee came out and daubed at the sweat streaming from his wrinkled face. "Hot, ain't it?" he said, and led the horse away.

Wilder walked down the street to the saloon. Ward Cox stood alone at the bar and Jim ordered a beer. Cox turned his head and said: "Buchard drive over yet?"

"A few head," Wilder admitted, and lifted the glass of warm beer.

"A few head too many," Cox stated. "I know that man. He showed what he was when he rode on Rayburn. There never was any definite proof again' the man . . . just in Walt's mind."

"He's got ambition," Wilder agreed, and leaned on the bar as if he were suddenly tired.

Heat lay heavily in the room and the smell of beer and stale sawdust was strong and rancid. He felt the unreasonable anger against it all rising and pushed it down, straightening his face so that it wouldn't show. He tried to rationalize it in his mind. Cursing the heat was like a small boy hitting the screen door because the wind blew it and smashed his finger. Wilder was determined not to be like that.

"I don't trust Philmore, either," Cox said. "He rode with Buchard when they hung Rayburn, didn't he? He's out after his cut, too, don't think he ain't."

"We're all in bad shape," Wilder said patiently. "There's no need to pick at one another."

Cox spoke as if he hadn't heard. "Come right down to it . . . I never liked Philmore. I always distrusted a man who hid his mouth behind a lot of whiskers."

Wilder turned his head to give him a long, unbelieving stare. Cox met his eyes with a stubborn intolerance. "Why tell me about it?" Wilder said softly. "Tell it to O.B. Philmore."

"Don't think I won't," Cox said acidly, and finished his beer. He turned and tapped Jim Wilder on the chest. "While I'm at it, I'll tell you a thing or two. My little girl came home cryin' last night."

"She's the kind that cries easy," Jim said, and held the man's eyes.

The bartender stopped stacking bottles to listen.

Cox stiffened, but lowered his voice to a dangerous softness. "Wilder, I know you. You're soft. Buchard knows it . . . we all know it. You ain't gonna last up there in the breaks, and, if I find out that you've hurt my little girl, then I'll run you out myself."

"All the hurt's in Emmaline's mind," Wilder said, then turned away from the man and finished his beer. Cox stared at him with an open disgust, then snorted and left the saloon.

Evening came and the clouds to the northeast built up until they towered like white mountains, rolling and boiling and carrying the promise of rain. Heat lightning shattered the darkness with quick streaks as Wilder walked to the Grange Hall at the end of Buster Street.

The musicians played listlessly to a handful of dancers who braved the sultry heat. Wilder saw Emmaline Cox in a corner and held out his hand. She rose silently, even thankfully, and followed him around the floor. He tried to draw her closer as they danced, but she put a small pressure against his chest and he abandoned the idea. He moved toward a door and, when she made no objection, led her out into the night.

Perspiration stood out in shining drops on her face, making bright streaks as it rolled off of her cheeks. In the distance thunder boomed, deep and rolling as it rebounded from the land. She pressed both hands to her hot cheeks and murmured: "Is there no end to this? If it doesn't get cooler, I think I'll go crazy."

"It'll rain," Wilder said, and the assurance in his voice brought her head up quickly.

"Why is it that you hold yourself so tight? I never know what you're thinking any more."

"You never did know," Wilder said, but there was no sting in his words. He rolled a smoke with a slow care and a match flared as he touched it to the twisted end.

Emmaline said softly: "Jim, I don't think I ever knew you at all."

"No," he said. "You never did."

He took her arm and they went back into the hall. The wall was still between them and he knew it would never come down. He wondered if she would ever discover this truth for herself.

Walt Buchard came in at eight and his shirt was damp and sticking to his heavy torso. Jim Wilder leaned against the far wall, talking to Virginia Philmore when the big man threaded his way through the chattering crowd and touched him on the arm. The heaviness of his temper was still boldly on his face and he said: "Wilder, tomorrow my beef is gonna drink your water hole dry."

"We'll talk about it in the morning," Jim said softly, and turned to Virginia.

Buchard wasn't the kind of a man who liked to be cut off like that and he took Wilder's shoulder and spun him around. Jim knocked the hand off and said easily: "Whoa, there, Walt. Don't start trouble in here." His voice was soft but flecks of temper stood out clearly in his eyes.

"What am I supposed to do?" Buchard said in a tight voice. "Sit still and let the rest of my herd die? Nothing bothers you. You're like a damn' Indian. It was a mistake ever to let you move into the breaks."

The crowd grew quiet to hear this and eyes turned to them expectantly. Outside, the thunder built up in volume, crashing and echoing, then dying to be taken up by another clap that rattled windows.

The sound ate into Buchard's tight nerves and he lashed out suddenly, rocking Wilder's head with a knotted fist. The heavy man's teeth were tightly together when he spoke as if he feared the thing rising in him. "Damn you, Wilder . . . I'll break that pokerface if I have to break your neck to do it. I'm coming in tomorrow . . . you hear?"

"Bring your gun with you, then," Wilder said, and didn't bother to wipe the trickle of blood from his chin. He keened the air like a dog, sniffing, then the others caught it and there was a sudden babbling as they tried to make it out.

Wilder shouted: "That's rain you smell! Rain!"

The crowd stampeded for the door and stood there as the first swollen drops struck the thick dust. The dust flew out and up, leaving a small, scooped-out bowl of moisture. Then other drops fell and dust rose above the ground like thin smoke as water beat upon it, soaking into the parched earth as fast as it fell.

It was a strong smell in the air and men stood out in it, letting it soak their clothes, letting it stream hair down over their foreheads. It worked on them as it did the land, giving them a new life just as the hope for life faded.

Virginia took Jim Wilder's arm and leaned her head against it, listening to the sound of it cascading from the gutted eaves. The splatter of it striking the ground filled the air with a faint roaring, but it was something each of them had longed to hear.

They turned back inside, leaving the doors and windows open to welcome the coolness that came with the rain. Buchard and Philmore looked at each other and some of the tension left their faces. The band played with more enthusiasm, although with the same melodious unconcern, the sudden coolness inducing the dancers into activity.

Wilder took Virginia in his arms and they moved out onto the floor. He held her close and she didn't seem to mind. He heard a man laugh and he stopped. It was a strange sound. He had not heard it in six months. Then he found that laughter was in him, too, and he gave her his twisted smile, moving toward the door.

She stopped at the threshold and said: "You

went out with one girl tonight. I don't know's I ought to go."

Behind her words was that luring fire, pulling at him as it had always done.

He smiled at her with his eyes and said: "You don't miss anything, do you?"

She shook her head and it stirred her dark ringlets into a dancing motion. They found shelter under the small porch and watched the rain come down.

"It's a glorious thing, isn't it?" She turned to him, close enough for him to smell the scented soap and the freshness she never lost for him. She laid a hand against his chest and the heat from her palm soaked through his shirt. "Would you have taken a gun to Walt in the morning?"

"We'll never know," Wilder said. "It's raining now. He'll have his own water." His voice was soft and withholding from her. It troubled her because he saw the flicker of it in her eyes when she moved and lamplight struck her face.

She was still close to him and desire rose in his eyes. She saw it, but didn't shy away from it and he took hope, drawing her to him. It was a short kiss, but it lacked nothing for him. There was a modest reserve to her, but the sweetness was there; the life bubbled below the surface of her full lips. He felt an answering desire stir her and it satisfied him because he was a patient man.

He said: "Maybe I shouldn't have done that, Virginia."

"I would have been insulted if you hadn't," she told him honestly, and turned to go back into the hall.

Buchard and her father still stood in the corner, talking in low tones. Jim glanced around the room until he found Ward Cox, but the man swung his eyes away. Wilder smiled to himself, knowing that Cox was retracting a few things in his mind. He saw Walt Buchard looking at him heavily and threaded his way through the dancers until he came up to the man.

Jim said plainly—"Just so you don't get any ideas about how I'm put together."—and hit Buchard flushly on the mouth.

The man staggered from the blow. He raised his hand and touched his split lip. He swung his balance forward as if to pursue the fight, then relaxed and said: "I had that one coming, Wilder."

Some of the dancers stopped at the sound of the blow and Buchard grew nervous and self-conscious at this attention. He turned quickly and walked to the door, snatching his hat from a wall peg as he passed by it.

O.B. Philmore waited until the man left. "You just bought a heap of trouble, Wilder . . . a powerful lot of trouble."

"I didn't ask for it," Jim stated. "Did you expect me to let it slide by?"

"Been better if you had," O.B. opined, then fished a large watch from his pocket. "Gettin' late. Never thought I'd enjoy a buggy ride in the rain, but danged if I ain't gonna tonight." He left Wilder to recover his daughter from the frantic embrace of a young cowpuncher who whirled her around the dance floor.

Emmaline Cox glanced at him and the young man moved toward her. "Leaving now?" he asked, not understanding the sulkiness around her mouth.

He saw then that she intended to ignore him, but she changed her mind and said: "She had an advantage out there in the rain." Jim looked at her with some amazement and she bit her lip, sorry she had permitted herself to slip.

"I didn't know that it made a damn, Emma."

"What do you know?" she flared. "You never let yourself out. What can you know about anyone else or how they feel? How can you?" She made a futile gesture with her hands as if she had been caught up in an emotion stronger than her will and wished to be free of it.

"I think we've both made bad guesses," Jim told her, and moved away. She followed him with her eyes until he walked out with Virginia Philmore, then her face changed and resentment rose to smother her beauty.

Ward Cox detached himself from the others and put his arm around Emmaline's shoulders. He stared at Wilder's retreating back and said: "Don't fret about it, honey. He's a proud man and they fall pretty hard. After he's down, you can have him on your terms."

"I don't think I'd want him that way," she murmured, and turned away to get her coat.

Rain fell in thick sheets and Wilder hitched up Philmore's buggy while Virginia and her father waited under the protection of the small porch. People called to each other and rigs slithered around in the mud as they turned shortly and wheeled out of the yard.

Wilder tied his horse to the back and climbed in. A few minutes later they rattled out of Warpaint. Virginia's white party dress was soaked through and molded against her, but she didn't seem to mind. He dropped her off at O.B.'s ranch around midnight, declined a hot cup of coffee, and rode into the breaks toward his own solitary place a few minutes later.

III

The morning dawned, chill and gray, announcing the commencement of another weeping day. Wilder looked out the door while his coffee boiled and saw no sign of a let-up. He finished a thin breakfast, sloshed through the mud to saddle his horse.

An hour later he cut out of the breaks and across the drenched flatness to Ward Cox's place. Water began to run sluggishly through the cuts draining the land and he splashed through, coming out a little later by Cox's barn.

Cox came out when he stopped by the porch and dismounted. Wilder wore an old slicker and water poured from the V crease in his hat. He took it off and slapped it against his chaps.

Cox grinned and said: "I feel like a new man."

"Water makes a difference," Wilder agreed, and looked at the swollen clouds boiling low overhead.

Cox's smile faded and he said bluntly: "You don't seem glad about it."

"So it's wet," Wilder said. "It don't make my herd grow . . . yours, either. When it stops, we'll still be broke."

Cox snorted and said: "How's your basins fillin' up? Must be near' full by now."

"Never looked," Jim stated. "I'll look in a day or two." He nodded toward the interior of the house. "Emmaline at home?"

"In the kitchen," Cox said. "Go on in." He stared a long time at Wilder's back even after the door closed behind him.

Emmaline turned from the sink and her face was stiff with her thoughts. Jim touched her on the shoulder and, when she didn't pull away, put his arm around her

"Emma," he said, "we shouldn't quarrel. It's

raining like the devil, but I wondered if you'd like to take a ride over to the Philmores with me. You don't get away much."

She thought of his out-of-the-way ride here and it overrode a flashing resentment. "I'll change my clothes," she said, and went down the hall to her room.

Wilder had a saddle horse waiting for her when she came out of the house. She swung up, and they rode from the yard. She wore a raincoat and pants, with a square of oilcloth over her head and pinned under her chin. She waited until they crossed the creek before speaking.

"Why did we quarrel last night, Jim?" Her voice was small and he realized how much it cost her to say this.

"Maybe we didn't," he said. "People sometimes build things up in their mind that's more real than the real thing."

She kicked her horse with her heels, turning him so that she faced him. She leaned from the saddle until her rain-streaked face was but a few inches from his. "What happened between us, Jim? From the first day you saw her, it changed between us . . . I could feel it change."

He shook his head. "The change was in your mind, Emma. It wasn't real to be changed."

It broke through her reserve, making her desperate. She said with a faint huskiness: "Kiss me, Jim."

He brought her against him with a force that half lifted her from the saddle. Her lips pressed against his and her arms tightened around him, but he felt a coolness, a detachment emanating from her even as their lips met. It was that deep reluctance to reveal herself, to place her love in any man's hands. He had always felt it when he was near her, and now he understood that she was incapable of loving.

The kiss carried no fire and no life; she drew away, knowing it contained no hope. Her face settled again, patient and slightly dogged. Her voice contained a deadness he had never heard before.

"Thank you, Jim. But I think it's harder now, knowing for sure, than it was not knowing and just hoping." She tried to smile and tears mingled with the rain on her face. "I think I'll go back home now."

He didn't say he was sorry; he spared her that humiliation. She turned the horse and lashed it into a mud-splattering run, riding with her head down and her shoulders rounded. Wilder let out a long, ragged breath and urged the horse into motion. Somehow he felt free.

Philmore and his daughter saw him riding across the flatness and waited on the porch. Jim dismounted and they went into the house. Jim sat at the kitchen table with a sprawled looseness and took the coffee Virginia handed him.

Jim said: "Your creek fillin' any lately, O.B.?"

The old man shook his head. "Be another three days yet. I guess I can stand the waitin' as long as I know it's comin'." He lifted his coffee cup, brushing his mustache back with his finger. "How's the water up at your place?"

"Runnin' in, I guess," Jim said, and lapsed into a pointed silence.

Philmore fidgeted in his chair and glanced at his daughter. He studied his blunt fingers a moment, then said: "I guess I spoke pretty tough the last time you was here, boy. I hope you ain't holdin' it against a man."

"Depends," Jim stated, "if you still mean it or not." He folded his hands behind his head and leaned back in his chair.

O.B. scowled. "Hell, the damned heat got on my nerves, that's all."

"That's your story," Wilder said. "You talked like that a few years ago, too . . . right after Buchard came over and you rode on Howie Rayburn. If you want an excuse, just let this rain keep up. Water can drive you crazy, too."

Philmore left the table and went out on the front porch. He was in a generous mood today and wouldn't pick up the stick. Wilder smiled when he thought of it.

He crossed the room to Virginia and said: "Want to take a look around the country? We don't ride much any more."

Her face broke into an easy smile. "I'll get my slicker and hat."

They cut into the breaks a few minutes later.

Virginia said: "I don't know what it is, Jim, but somehow you seem different."

"I'm wet now," Wilder said. "I don't have to hold my breath any more."

She shook her head and water sloshed from her hat. "You know I don't mean that. The something that's always bothered you doesn't bother you any more."

She was the kind of a girl who wouldn't permit evasion. He had discovered that at their first meeting. She had an open frankness that called for an answering straightforwardness. He said: "I just came from the Cox's. There isn't anything between Emmaline and me. She knows it now."

He didn't try to kiss her, even as her eyes warmed and her lips turned full and inviting. She smiled and said barely above the spatter of the rain: "You're a faithful man, Jim. It's one of the things that made me love you so."

It was nothing he didn't already know although it was the first time she had ever spoken of it. It cemented them firmly for all time because they were unchanging people.

Jim laid his hand over hers and said: "I knew it would be like this from the start."

There was no more talk between them until

they came out of the rocks above his small ranch. They cut across a flat butte and into a basin a mile south of his place. Water gushed out of fissures, boiling and foaming its way into the scooped-out watershed. Already a pool thirty yards wide had formed and was rising hourly. They dismounted and took shelter in a shallow cave protected by a rock overhang. At some time before Wilder had cut and stacked brush inside and now he built a fire. Virginia crowded close to the heat and sat there, letting her pants legs steam.

Wilder looked at the basin and said: "I don't like it. Another day or two and this basin's gonna spill over. It'll run all over Buchard's place, maybe back up in the creek and wash some of your father's place out."

"We've had rain before."

"Not days on end of it," Jim said.

He rolled a smoke and listened to the water strike the rocks. The land was gray and angry-looking with the pelting rain bouncing, making a foot-high mist over the surface.

Virginia touched him on the arm and he swung his attention to the rider who eased his way out of the rocks and approached the basin. The man was bundled in oilskins, but his bulk was unmistakable even in the poor light. He caught sight of Wilder's small fire and moved over to them, dismounting with a deep grunt. He came in and slapped the water from his hat.

"Damn this rain anyhow," he said. "Ain't a damn' thing dry around here."

"Couple of days ago," Jim said, "you was complaining about it bein' dry and hot. Can't you make up your mind?"

"I like it a little between," Buchard said, and squatted by the fire. He gave Virginia a quick glance and said knowingly: "Kinda cozy in here, ain't it?"

"You tryin' to say something?" Wilder asked with surprising mildness.

"No," Walt admitted, and changed the subject. "I rode over to tell you that some water's comin' in my creek. I won't be needin' your water now."

"I figured that out," Wilder said, and poked at the fire with a short stick.

Buchard's heavy face came around and he stared at the man with a sudden belligerence. "Don't make trouble with me," he said. "I haven't forgot how you threw down on me once with a rifle. I've handled your kind before."

"You're gettin' touchy again," Wilder told him. "A week ago it was the heat . . . now it's the wet. What was it with Howie? Did you wonder if you could hang a man or not?"

He held Buchard's eyes and saw that the man wanted to take it up, but something held him. He made a cutting motion with his hand and turned to his horse. A moment later he vanished in the slanting rain.

Wilder kicked the fire to scattered ashes and helped Virginia into her rain gear. They mounted and rode to the seep near his cabin. Water came to within a foot of the top and Wilder knew it would go on rising.

He said: "I don't like this at all. Tomorrow it'll be running down into the flats and swellin' the creek."

He stabled the horses in his barn and they crossed the muddy yard. He opened the door for her, but she swung around to face him and stepped close. "I've waited long enough," she said, and laced her arms around his neck.

It was the kind of a kiss that a lonely man dreams of and he felt an uncalled fire rising in him. They broke apart and she smiled before stepping into the cabin

He watched her as she looked around and knew what was going on in her mind. She ran her hand over the table top and back of the chair with a familiarity she had never dared before. Wilder said: "Can you be happy here?"

"Very," she said simply, and he turned away from her, not trusting himself, and lighted the fire.

There was no let-up on the third day and Wilder rose early to inspect his basins. He didn't like it at all. The seep in back of his cabin was spilling itself down the rough defiles to the creek below.

He saddled hurriedly and rode to Ward Cox's ranch.

Cox was in a surly frame of mind. He said: "Damn water anyhow! My men can't get around in this gumbo. I lost a good saddle horse yestiddy from a fall."

"We're in trouble," Wilder said, "unless this rain lets up." He explained about the water backing up above his place. Cox listened with a great deal of attention and it was then that Wilder understood the man. Cox liked trouble. He welcomed it because it gave him a chance to empty the acid of his spleen onto the world without fear of consequence. Wilder doubted if the man could have lived without this outlet.

"Get your horse," Jim said. "We'll ride to Philmore's and hash it out. I don't mean to sit around with my hands folded and get washed out."

Cox agreed, and a few minutes later they were cutting across the rain-swollen land. The creek was higher when they crossed it, and Cox said: "Damn it all. If it don't blow a man away, it drowns him. Who the hell regulates the damned weather anyway?"

Wilder kicked down a reply and they rode on, coming out through Philmore's back pasture an hour later. Walt Buchard's horse was in the yard when they dismounted and clomped across the porch. Philmore broke off his talk when they entered the room. He and Buchard each had a whiskey, and O.B. offered one to Wilder, pointedly ignoring Cox.

Wilder said: "The water's backin' up behind my place."

"Don't tell me your troubles," O.B. said flatly. "I got enough of my own."

"You're in for some more," Jim stated. "When that water lets go, it'll flood all of you out down here. The creeks ain't big enough to carry it away that fast."

Buchard scowled and said: "You been a hex up there, Wilder. If I'd had my way, you'd been on the same rafter as Rayburn."

"You didn't make it then," Jim said. "What makes you think you could make the grade now?" He turned his head as Virginia came into the room. Something warm and close passed between them and everyone saw it, but Wilder didn't care. He said: "There's one thing we can do, but we'll have to do it now . . . dynamite those basins and let them spill when the creek's low enough to handle it. It may save a complete washout later."

Buchard slapped his leg and his mouth was puckered. "Why, damn you, Wilder! I'll get the biggest blast from that. I'll lose my outbuildings for sure."

"Better to lose a few now than wait until it's too late and lose 'em all."

"You sit up there, high and dry," Cox said. "I

45

see through you, Wilder. You always wanted to hit back at us because of Rayburn and this is your chance. You hurt my girl . . . now you want to hurt me. You try anything, and, by God, I'll put a bullet in you!"

Wilder's temper made flecks in his eyes, but he kicked it in place. He stated: "I'm buying dynamite tonight. I'm gonna bleed those basins and nobody better try and stop me."

Walt Buchard couldn't ignore a challenge, even a veiled one, and took a step forward.

Wilder slid his hand in the pocket slit of his rain cape. "I got a gun here. Don't make me use it." The tone of his voice held them and he motioned to Virginia. "Hitch up your father's buckboard."

She turned to get her hat and O.B.'s intolerant voice boomed in the room. "Go with him now, and there ain't no comin' back!"

"I have no intention of coming back," Virginia said, and went out.

Wilder held them quietly with his hand under his slicker, then backed out of the door when he heard the slosh of the team. No one moved. Then he was off of the porch, in the buckboard, riding hurriedly from the yard.

Virginia drove in silence while he turned his head frequently and studied the road behind them. She said: "Would you really have shot?"

"I think I would have," Wilder admitted. "I

never allowed myself the luxury of getting mad before, but I'm at the end of my rope, too. When that seep goes, my place'll go out with it."

"I never knew it before, but Father and Cox are afraid of you. They won't try to stop you, Jim."

"Walt Buchard will try," Wilder stated, and studied his hands. "You shouldn't have come, Virginia. I had no right to ask you."

She snorted. "You have every right. I wouldn't have let you go without me."

IV

They turned into Warpaint in the early afternoon. Water came off of the roofs in thick, transparent sheets and mud stood fetlock deep in the street. Water ran, churning and brown, in the gutters, lapping over the boardwalks in places where heavy cross traffic had broken them down. They pulled in at the hardware store and Jim got down, handing Virginia to the shelter of the awning.

Rad Dickenson looked up quickly when they came in and Wilder said: "Give me four boxes of blasting sticks and a dozen caps." Outside a horse splashed hurriedly down the street and a rider swung off out of Wilder's vision. The sound of it sent a shot of warning through him and he slapped the counter. "Hurry up, man! I don't have all day!"

Dickenson carried them out of the back room, one by one, and placed them evenly on the counter. Wilder felt the tightness within him building and tried to beat it down, but it was too strong. It blossomed as a full-blown temper and he wanted to strike out with his fists.

His knuckles bounced off of the counter and he snapped: "Damn this rain!"

Virginia's head came around quickly, a sudden alarm in her eyes.

After the caps were laid on the counter, Dickenson said: "That'll be sixteen dollars and thirty-four cents."

"Charge it to the good of the country," Wilder told him, and lifted two boxes at a time. His voice had suddenly turned wild and tight and Dickenson didn't argue, although the thought was plain on his face. Wilder stowed it in the buckboard and covered it with a tarp.

Two more riders pounded through the mud at the end of the street and Wilder lifted Virginia into the rig as they halted. Cox and Philmore swung down as a man stepped out of a gap between the buildings three doors down. He turned when Buchard called his name in a driving voice: "Wilder!"

Virginia took his arm, but he shook her off and stepped away from the buckboard, his hand sliding into the slit of his slicker. Suddenly he was eager to fight and knew with a shocking

48

clarity that it was a long sought-after thing.

Buchard closed the distance to thirty feet and said: "Wilder, I never should have let you get this far."

The heavy man stood, flat-footed, with that great intolerance across his heavy face. His left hand lifted and fingered the dangling thong of his dripping hat, and, when the hand dropped, Wilder shot through the folds of his slicker.

Sound bucketed up and down the street, twisted by the slanting wind. The bullet caught Buchard with his gun half drawn, spinning him and slamming him into the mud. Philmore and Cox ran to him, half lifting him and pulling him to the questionable shelter of a building overhang.

Wilder stood rooted while people boiled out of the buildings lining the street. Buchard pawed weakly at the blood oozing from his side. The doctor dashed from his upstairs office across the street, his black coat flapping, his bag swinging from the end of a skinny arm.

Philmore left the wounded man and pushed his way through the crowd. He stopped before Wilder and said: "You thought you was above it, didn't you? All right . . . go dynamite them damned basins. No one'll stop you."

Wilder had an answer but something held him and it was a moment before he understood what it was.

Rain no longer pelted the crown of his hat.

The water slacked from the slanting roofs, dripping in smaller streams, then stopped altogether. A sound was lifted from the land, leaving in its wake a broad silence. Men stopped talking and looked around as the sky lightened and a wide shaft of sunlight fell, golden and sparkling, in the mud.

Philmore said—"I'll be damned."—and the words shook Wilder free of his thoughts. He shouldered past the older man and elbowed his way through the crowd to kneel by Walt Buchard.

"Get you bad?"

Buchard's voice was weak. "Naw. I never thought you'd shoot, Wilder."

"You was ready to shoot me."

"I'd 'a' hung you once, too," Buchard said. "But you pointed that damn' rifle at my gut. I guess you ain't much different from Cox or any of the others. I just never saw it before, that's all."

Wilder stood up when the doctor pushed at him, then stood aside as four men lifted Buchard on a table leaf, carrying him across the street. The crowd broke up into chattering segments and he turned back to the buckboard. He threw the gun in the back and leaned heavily against the wheel.

Virginia said nothing, just ran her hand through his wet hair, and everyone saw the caress and understood it. Dickenson came out of his store to stand and study the sun-bathed street. He said to no one in particular: "It's hard to satisfy a man sometimes."

Wilder turned his head and gave him a long look.

"Guess you won't need the dynamite now," the man added, and carried it back into his store.

Philmore came back over and gave Wilder a look that was not unfriendly. He said to his daughter: "I didn't mean what I said, honey. I was riled."

"I know you didn't, but I'm not coming back. I have a life of my own."

The old man knew what she meant. He touched Wilder on the arm and murmured: "Life is sure hell to live sometimes." He crossed to his horse and mounted heavily, then rode out of town.

Sun bathed the land again, a hot sun that soon caused wisps of steam to rise from the mud. Rooftops dried in patches and the mood of the land changed. In a week it would be green. In a week men would curse the heat and pray for rain, and Wilder smiled because he knew he'd be cursing and praying, too.

THE CONTEST

From his kitchen window Charlie Runyon could look out at the vast and gray world. Dawn was a pink blush in the east and he studied the charcoal shadows of the ranch yard. The kitchen stove had not yet thrown out enough heat to push back the dawn chill. Outside, dew painted a tinfoil sparkle on the grass.

Charlie Runyon set the coffee pot on the stove and, while it thumped and rocked on a heat-warped bottom, gathered his blankets and rolled them. His packsack had been made up last night and was sitting by the door. He went into the bedroom for his rifle and a few spare cartridges.

Runyon drank his coffee black and scalding. Afterward he killed the fire and crossed to the barn where he kept his jeep. He stowed the gear in the back and made a last-minute check. Rope, a small block and tackle—he had everything he needed, including the hunting license pinned to his battered hat.

From across the valley a pinpoint of light twinkled like a distant star and Charlie Runyon's sharply chiseled face settled. Harry Clymer was getting ready for the hunt. Starting his jeep,

Charlie Runyon backed out of the barn and drove across the yard, heading straight across the flat pasture. Five gates later he turned right on the county road. A glance back showed a pair of headlights cutting the dawn's gray half light. *Damn Harry Clymer anyway,* Runyon thought, and increased his speed.

Leaving the county road, Runyon followed a slash through the woods. There was enough light now to see without his headlights and he switched them off. Passing one camp of hunters, he waved, but did not stop.

He ground up a steep logging road, long abandoned and now overgrown with third-year brush. Manzanita and chamisal whipped the hood and fenders, and he stopped to put up the windshield, then drove on.

Vehicle tracks reminded him that others had recently traveled this way, but this caused Runyon no concern. Reaching the table top of this mountain, Runyon drove across to a camp where three men sat around a fire. The high air was like an ice pick through his blanket-lined jacket and he could see his breath. Frost turned the foliage to aluminum.

One of the men hunkering down by the fire held out a tin cup and indicated the coffee pot. "You're early this year," he said. "Clymer behind you?"

"Not far," Runyon said, and squatted. He was a

lean, work-hammered man in his late twenties. His hair was fawn-colored and beneath the thickets of his eyebrows slate-gray eyes moved quickly. Charlie Runyon sipped his coffee. "Any luck, Doc?"

"Pete jumped a forked-horn shortly after dawn," Doc said. "He's hanging over there."

Runyon's eyes traveled to the trees where two men stuffed grass into the opened belly of a deer. They came back to the fire and opened their palms to the blaze. Blood made splotches on their tan trousers. The back of one man's hands was covered with blood, now dry and cracked in the seams of his joints.

From the trail below came the snorting of a truck's exhaust and Runyon's face settled slightly. Pete said: "Harry Clymer's Dodge. You and Harry going to hunt together, Charlie?"

"Not likely," Runyon said.

"Charlie's feud with the buck is private," Doc said, chopping off his talk as Clymer worked his truck across the clearing and got out. He was a heavy man, round-faced with bland eyes, but the blandness was a veil behind which other emotions simmered. Unlike Runyon, Clymer was clean-shaven, but the density of his whiskers gave his jaw a bluish cast. He helped himself to the coffee pot without invitation and made a place for himself at the fire. The two men standing continued to warm their hands while Doc remained silent.

Carefully Clymer laid his scope-mounted .30-06 beside him. He glanced at Runyon over the rim of the cup and said: "You must have got up at midnight, Charlie."

"I didn't stop to shave," Runyon said.

Clymer frowned. "Let's make a bet, Charlie," he said softly.

"I never bet," Runyon said. "Too much trouble collecting."

Harry Clymer's frown deepened and he sloshed coffee around in his cup. "A real deal, Charlie. You admit that buck's too smart for you and I'll get him. You won't have to be bothered." He laughed, and drained his cup. "He's trampled your garden, killed your dog, and gored a horse to where you had to shoot him." Clymer shook his head slowly. "No, sir, Charlie, that buck's got you buffaloed."

"This year I'll get him," Runyon said. "I know his tricks."

Doc chuckled and packed his pipe. "I don't think Charlie wants him as bad as he lets on. If he did, he'd have shot him from the back porch."

Runyon's head came up and he looked at this man. "I want him right enough," he said. He scraped a hand across his face and glanced up at the sky. A high layer of thin clouds was a gauze through which the sun filtered. "There's weather coming. He'll come out then. He always does."

"He's teasing you," Pete said. "Charlie, you and

that buck got too much respect for one another to kill over it."

"I got that all right," Runyon admitted.

"Sure be a shame," Clymer said, "if one of the boys shot him, wouldn't it?" He smiled and his eyes were dark buttons. "You never hunt with me, Charlie. You afraid I'll shoot him?"

"I'm not afraid of that," Runyon said. His big hands rested on his knees, the fingers splayed.

Clymer looked at the other men. Their eyes were watchful. "These boys have a gentleman's agreement not to shoot him," he said. "But I never felt that way. You ever wonder why, Charlie?"

"I guess you got your reasons," Runyon said. He raised his eyes and scanned the faces around the fire. Then he looked at Harry Clymer.

"We'll go out together," Clymer said, smiling. "I'll take the north side of Bugle Peak and you can come in from the south. We'll work him onto the flats where I can reach him with the Thirty-Aught-Six."

Runyon stood up. He took out a cigarette and rolled it between his fingers a moment before lighting it. "I'll go alone," he said.

"Afraid of getting beat by a better man?" Clymer asked. He waved this aside. "Forget it, Charlie. I'm going in your direction, so I'll pack in with you."

Runyon said nothing. He took his pack and .30-40 Krag from the jeep and started across the

56

clearing. Clymer winked at the others, and followed him. In the distance Bugle Peak pushed rocky shoulders higher than the surrounding range. There was a mantle of snow on the top and a high altitude wind whipped it away in a streak to the east. Runyon followed the breaks and traveled fast. Behind him, Clymer's rubber-soled boots fractured twigs. There was no talk between these men.

During the afternoon, Runyon worked his way along the ridges, always angling toward Bugle Peak. There were no hunters here for the terrain was outlandishly rough and the traveling diffi-cult. The day was without warmth, yet Runyon shed his jacket. Harry Clymer stayed on Runyon's heels and several times Runyon heard Clymer's heavy breathing. Runyon chose the little-known trails that led off these high ridges and into the wild cañons below.

That night Runyon camped at the base of Bugle Peak. He made a small fire and fixed his meal, cooking the coffee in the skillet. Clymer said: "You wouldn't ask a man to share a fire, would you?"

"I'd ask a man," Runyon said evenly. He saw the stain of anger in Clymer's face. "Fix your own meal," he said, leaning back to enjoy his cigarette. "Tomorrow I'm leaving early. You go your own way."

"My way is with you," Clymer said. "You wouldn't try to stop me, would you, Charlie?" He forked bacon into his mouth.

"What's this to you?" Runyon asked. "What are you butting in for?"

"I like to see a man in action," Clymer said. "Proud ones like you give me a bellyache." He patted his scope-mounted rifle. "I'm not the hunter you are, Charlie, but I'm going to beat you to him. I can take my shot from four, five hundred yards. That gives me an edge over you, don't it?"

"The only one you ever had," Runyon said. "Is that what bothers you?"

Clymer frowned while Runyon shook out his blankets. He rolled in and turned his back to the fire. Clymer moved around with an animal restlessness, then settled down for the night.

Runyon woke hours before dawn. The wind had picked up and a solid layer of clouds made a tent over the land. He kindled the fire. His shoulders were stiff from the cold and he spread his hands to the heat, rubbing them briskly. Clymer stirred and, when he saw the fire, got up and hunkered down across from Runyon.

"You thinking of giving me the slip, Charlie?"

"Quick as I drink my coffee," Runyon said, and rolled his gear. He made his coffee and drank it, then shouldered his pack and struck out.

Clymer was not ready and he shouted after

Runyon: "You think you're god-damned smart, don't you!"

Two hours later Runyon was in a high, rocky pocket that commanded a dry wash. He sat with his shoulders hunched against the cold ripping off the flanks of Bugle Peak. Since he had taken that first shot at the buck five years ago, Runyon had been over this mountain so often that he was familiar with every cañon, every vague trail that criss-crossed it.

He had been repairing the fence on his west section the day he had seen the buck. From his nearby jeep he took his rifle and shot, but the buck jumped too quickly, went down, then got up immediately, and was gone by the time Runyon had worked the bolt.

From that day forward a personal war existed, declared first by the deer. He had been irritated by the small depredations and had blamed it on coyotes until he saw the buck's tracks in the rutabaga patch.

With almost human intellect the deer sought revenge for that wound. And just as savagely, Charlie Runyon sought to slay the buck.

Runyon waited, chilled to the point of numbness. The wind moaned among the rocks, and he rested his back against a huge boulder. There was a faint flush to the east, the false dawn. He wondered where Clymer was, then told himself that he didn't give a damn, but he did. Clymer would shoot the buck merely to deny Runyon the pleasure. The man was like that.

Runyon was not aware of the particular thing that pinpointed his attention. Later, when he thought about it, he decided it was the natural awareness a man has for the enemy. He was alert now and in a moment saw the vague shape of the buck making his cautious way down the wash. Runyon waited. His downwind position was good. The range was close enough. He glanced at the sky as though he willed the dawn to break.

The shooting would be bad in this light and he needed a neck or heart shot to kill this proud animal. He decided to move and wondered if he could do this without alarming his quarry. Shouldering his pack, he left the shelter via a climbing route that took him high in the rocks. He had traveled fifty yards when his foot dislodged a small stone that sent up a wakeful clatter as it cascaded into the wash.

Snorting in surprise, the buck raced past Runyon before he could shoulder the rifle. Leaping boulders, the buck tore down the wash and disappeared around a bend. Runyon sat down wearily, the sharp sense of defeat like a weight on his back.

Then he heard the shot, the sharp, echoing slap of Clymer's .30-06 Springfield. This prodded Runyon into instant action. He dashed from his place and slid and ran toward the downside of the wash. The dawn was growing boldly now and night washed away as he ran on. He found Clymer there, but not the buck.

"I got him for you," Clymer said, and there was a swollen pride in his voice. "I was trailing you when he barreled through. He went down, but got up. We can track him by the blood."

Runyon's first impulse was to hit him, but he pushed this aside and struck out with Clymer following. Three minutes later he saw a crimson patch on a small rock and, when he found another thirty yards farther down trail, established his direction and increased his pace.

The weather contained a raw bite, and a glance upward at the mountain walls told him that it was snowing heavily in the high camps. Thick, rolling clouds hung like a dirty tarp over the range, and, within an hour, it began to rain, a cold, near-snow mist that put an ache in a man's bones.

By mid-morning the buck had not been found although Runyon was certain he was on the right trail. Clymer had no heart for this and made grumbling comments but Runyon did not answer him. By early afternoon the rain was so heavy that Runyon trailed by guess. Clymer said: "You crazy fool! Don't you have sense enough to quit?"

"I finish what I start," Runyon said. Water poured from the crease in his hat and his denims were plastered soggily against his body.

"And I never do, is that it?" Clymer's teeth

were clenched against the chill. "You trying to rub my face in it?"

"You do that yourself," Runyon said. "Go on back if you want. You can make it by dark if you don't sit down too much." He raised a hand to paw water from his face. Exposure was turning it into wrinkled crêpe. "You're even a lousy shot, Harry."

Runyon watched Clymer, his body relaxed, his pale eyes fastened on Clymer's face. "You're crazy!" Clymer said, and wheeled. A moment later the veil of rain swallowed him up, and Runyon went on. He knew where he was and turned left, following a finger cañon into very rough country. The deer, he decided, would hole up. They rarely moved around during the day, and with a bullet wound he would soon seek a bed.

Nightfall caught Runyon in a dead-end, and he camped beneath a rock overhang while the rain whipped a waterfall over a nearby watercourse. The dead brush he gathered was too soggy for a hot fire and he rolled into his wet blankets. He lay there, listening to the roaring drum of the rain and thought about another time when he went out and found his rutabaga patch ruined. When a man started from scratch on two barren sections, he counted his profits carefully, and the loss of his rutabagas was a financial blow. Walking over the ruin, Runyon had seen the buck's tracks and there began the festering sore of revenge in his mind.

"I'll get him this year," he said to the rain, and went to sleep.

In the morning Runyon beat the dawn. The rain had not slackened. He built a small fire and made his coffee and, when the first streaks of gray lightened the sky, started out. Through this weeping day he traced another cañon to the end. That night he spent sitting in the rain for he could find no shelter. In spite of the cold he dozed and dreamed.

". . . Ninety dollars to fix her up, Charlie," the garage man was saying, and Runyon looked again at the damage the buck had done to his jeep. The night before he had heard a calf complaining. His headlights had picked up the buck thirty yards from the fence. His rifle was in the house and the buck sensed this for he charged. Animal and machine battled. In the end the buck left the field while Runyon watched the water pour from the ruined radiator. One headlight was dead. A tire was ripped. The windshield was smashed and the hood buckled where the buck had slashed it with his forefeet. . . .

The ache in his knees woke him and he drew the wet blanket tighter. The cold had increased until the rain turned to melting snow. He remembered that he had been dreaming and thought about the peaches—$2,000 worth of ruined peaches.

A man was a fool, he decided, to try ranching alone. There was too much to do. Not having the money to hire pickers, he had scattered straw beneath the trees to cushion the dropping fruit. This would cost him five percent of the crop in bruises, but it was cheaper than pickers.

Cheaper until the buck entered the orchard and trampled over half of the yield. Runyon had to borrow money from the bank to tide him over because of this.

"Why didn't I just get a nuisance permit and shoot him?" he asked the snow. This had occurred to him before and he could find no satisfactory answer. Somehow it did not seem right to Charlie Runyon to shoot such a bold and magnificent enemy in such a low manner. He could not shoot anything in the back.

He stood up and put his blankets away and in the darkness began to work his way toward the mouth of the cañon. At the end of the fourth day Charlie Runyon supposed that no one would question him if he returned to the jeep and admitted defeat. He felt ashamed that his misery would turn and allow such a thought to enter his head. With a terrible and savage determination he went on. He intended to go on until he found the buck dead or killed it with his own bullet.

At the end of the week the snow stopped. Runyon knew a week had gone by for he had been making small nicks in his rifle stock. These notches separated one miserable day from another. With no more snow to pester him, he enjoyed his first hot meal that evening. He sat naked before the blistering blaze while his clothes dried.

Then he slept.

At dawn he told himself that he would backtrack up the wash. A sense of defeat dogged him as it had every season these last four years. The buck was too much for him. He hated to admit this, but the facts were there. Slowly he worked his way upcañon toward the high ridges. His jeep was roughly eighteen miles east.

As he climbed higher, the snow became less soggy and at 4,000 feet was dry drifts, windrows of white that made progress hard labor. This slowed him and he decided to spend another night here, choosing for his campsite a small ravine that cut back a few hundred yards into the mountain's breast. There was timber here, stunted trees spaced by smaller shrubs. Runyon anticipated another small fire.

Then he found the buck.

The deer was in a bed at the base of a chamisal clump and Runyon halted. There were seventy yards between them. The buck raised his head, his eyes rolling.

Runyon shifted the Krag off his shoulder and worked the bolt. His heart was a heavy hammering in his chest and this irritated him.

With forefeet digging, the buck tried to rise, but could not. Runyon shouldered his rifle and observed the buck through the peep sight. The buck waited motionlessly. There was an awful dignity about the way he studied Runyon and Runyon began to shake. Here were the enemies, face to face at last. The deer waited and Runyon lowered the rifle, thumbed on the safety, and sat down on a rock.

Between these two lay a strange and indefinable code. He had had his chances before to shoot out of season but some sense of fairness had held him back. The buck seemed to understand this for Runyon could leave his place a month at a time and return to find tracks, but no damage done.

The buck only raided when he was at home. This was his challenge, the meeting of these two unbending animals, savage and proud, both driven by inflexible wills.

Charlie Runyon knew then that he would not shoot the buck. Not this way he wouldn't.

Full darkness was not an hour away when he returned to the mouth of the ravine. With his hatchet he felled small pines. Darkness did not stop him and he worked on into the night. For light he built a fire and the passage of time was unobserved. When morning came, he had erected a pole barricade across the ravine.

His enemy was sealed off.

He started down the draw again, walking rapidly toward the flatlands ten miles beyond. He paused at a neighbor's house and borrowed a pickup truck. At his own place he made up another pack. Bed sheets for bandages, carbolic salve, turpentine, a bucket, an extra coat, and three blankets, more food. He threw the heavy pack in the truck.

Runyon returned the pickup, thanked his neighbor, and started back toward Bugle Peak. Nightfall found him scaling the rocks that led into the ravine.

The buck was still there, raising his head while Charlie Runyon unloaded the two packs. He built a fire and cooked his supper, then approached the buck with a lariat looped and ready to throw. It took him better than an hour to snub the buck's head and hoofs, but he had a great deal of respect for a deer's stamina and he had no intention of dying here with a broken leg or bled out from cuts inflicted by razor-sharp hoofs.

The bullet had taken the buck in the neck, but low down, missing the windpipe and vein. Runyon cleaned out the matted, swollen wound and put carbolic salve on it, wrapping it tightly. The buck was frightened, but the ropes held him and Runyon was pleased that he could show this mercy to such an old enemy.

He slept two hours and woke shivering for the fire had died out. The wind was smart again and the promise of more weather was in the air. Building up his fire, Runyon began to cut timber and by midnight had fallen enough to notch into a three-sided lean-to. By morning he had a solid branch roof covering it and stood beneath it to watch the fall of new snow.

The next day he erected a baffle wall to reflect heat from the fire. He kept the deer tied and changed the dressing twice. On the third night the snow stopped falling. There was nearly two feet of it on the ground. Runyon built up his fire, intending to brew some coffee. The buck snorted and Runyon went to him when he heard the flat, hacking cough.

The buck did not prick up his ears when Runyon entered. The eyes were half closed and the lids seemed thick. Crusts of mucus stuck in the corners. The deer coughed again and a stream of phlegm ran from his nose.

Runyon did not know much about doctoring a deer, but he knew how "strangles" began with a horse. He cut two stout poles and spent considerable time inserting them in the roof. With rope and blankets he made a double sling and hoisted the deer. Runyon didn't want him to strangle.

The deer stood with head dropped, and, when he coughed, his ribs fluctuated like the seams of an accordion. Wind whistled in the buck's nose.

Runyon heated a bucket of water and added

turpentine and carbolic salve. The buck did not want to inhale this steaming brew, but Runyon forced it on him, offering silent apologies while he did so.

He was the enemy and showing mercy and he knew how this proud animal's pride suffered to have to accept it. The buck grew quiet and the breathing was less labored. Runyon kept at this until his arms throbbed from holding the bucket. He paused to reheat the water and cut more wood for the fire. The night grew longer and more bitter, and near morning a fresh storm descended in howling fury. Wind battered at the shelter and spun snow into a whipping fog that stung like needles. Runyon had no idea how cold it was, but his toes tingled and his heavy coat was none too warm. He needed sleep, dry clothes. All the blankets but two were covering the deer.

For the last day or so a dull ache had been hammering his skull and all food tasted badly now. Whiskers covered his face and he spent his time in constant attendance on the deer.

Work never ended for him. The fire ate wood at an alarming rate and medications had to be applied hourly lest the deer strangle. Runyon staggered when he walked and the buck's condition grew grave. The whistling was more pronounced and the deer drew painfully for air.

Charlie Runyon began to strop his knife on his boot.

The buck made no protest when Runyon felt for the windpipe. He pushed the point through the skin and blood spouted, covering his hand and sleeve. The buck reared slightly and Runyon gripped the ear, holding him while he cut a hole in the flesh.

Suddenly the buck's labored breathing ceased and he drew deep lungfuls of air. The bleeding abated, and Runyon sponged the spot with a cloth dipped in a mild carbolic solution. There was no sleep for him now and his eyes began to burn intolerably. He wondered why he didn't give up and decided the buck would have to die first. And he would prevent that if it was possible. Mucus drained from the hole and Runyon kept sponging it for it would have clogged in an hour's time had he not kept it wet.

Runyon could spend no more than fifteen minutes at a time for his meals. There was no sleep save what he could catch standing up and he was afraid of this because he might sleep too long. At the end of a week the storm had blown itself out and he knew that they were solidly hemmed in. The snow was banked to the top of the lean-to, but the temperature came up slightly.

He treated the buck's congestion by allowing the throat opening to clog slightly, forcing the deer to breathe through his nose. And when he did this, Runyon held steaming carbolic for the deer to breathe. Slowly at first, then more rapidly, the deer's condition improved. At last he could stand without the slings and Runyon dressed the neck opening, allowing it to heal.

With the last of his bacon gone—the flour sack had been emptied yesterday—Charlie Runyon doled out his remaining coffee. He was a badly worn man. Whiskers were two inches long on his face and deep lines were etched around his eyes. He knew the stain of this would stay with him, but he didn't care.

Now that the deer was improved, Runyon found himself with time on his hands. He used the frying pan for a shovel and began to dig a way out. This was backbreaking but he did not shirk it. He divided his time between shoveling snow and tending the deer.

Runyon climbed carefully to a high rock and looked down the draw. He saw them, three dark dots moving slowly toward Bugle Peak. He fired his rifle twice and listened to the bouncing echoes. Then he heard the answering shots.

They found his barricaded ravine three hours later and climbed the rocks to get in. Harry Clymer looked at the lean-to and said: "Everybody thought you were dead, Charlie."

One of the men began to stoke the fire and fix a meal. The flavors started saliva working in Runyon's jaws but he let none of this show on his face. All of the men saw the lean-to and knew that the buck was there, but no one asked him about it. Clymer kept his rifle by his side while he ate. Finally he could stand it no longer and got up.

Runyon said: "I wouldn't go in there, Harry."

"I walked up here," Clymer said. "I got a right to look."

"You don't have any rights," Runyon said, his drill-sharp eyes locked with Clymer's.

The round-faced man stood there for a moment, then made a disgusted motion with his hand. "That's the thanks a man gets. We come up here thinking you were hurt, maybe dying. Keep the god-damned deer!"

"I don't want to do that, either," Runyon said, and went to the lean-to. He led the buck out, shy and skittish now with these strange men here. At the barricade Runyon kicked until he loosened a pole, then used this to upset others. He slashed the rope holding the buck and allowed him to trot away. Twenty yards down the draw the deer paused and looked back, his magnificent head poised. Something passed between man and animal and Runyon smiled. "Get!" he said, and the buck dashed away with a snort.

When he turned toward the fire, he found Clymer standing, his rifle in his hands.

"What are you thinking about, Harry?" Runyon asked.

"I'll kill that deer yet," Clymer said tightly.

Runyon walked up to him and knocked the

rifle into the snow. Clymer made a grab for it, and Runyon gave him a shove that sent him sprawling. Then Runyon picked up the rifle and smashed it against a rock. The stock splintered and whipped around, still tethered by the sling. The scope broke free of the mount and bounded into the snow. Then Charlie Runyon threw the wrecked gun away from him and hunkered down by the fire. He did not look at Harry Clymer when he said: "Just leave him alone, Harry. You hear?"

The two men with Clymer looked at each other and maintained a strict neutrality. Clymer massaged his palms against his thighs. "After what he's done to you . . . you lost your mind?"

Runyon's head came up and his eyes were angry and impatient with this man's stupidity. "We're paid off, Harry! Can't you understand that? It's all over now!" He poured himself some coffee and sat with the cup under his nose, inhaling the strong flavor. "That smells good," he said softly. "Mighty good."

THE FAR-TRAVELIN' MAN

From the sagging porch of Deke Spears's store, Jethro Langtry could see a far piece down the dirt road, up to where it made a climb to the top of the hill and there turned and was hidden by the trees. Jethro was thirty some, not the brightest man in the village, but smart enough to know work didn't agree with him, so it was only natural that he'd be good at looking and listening,

He heard the car laboring up the blind side of the hill, and he took his hands from the bib of his overalls, turned his head, and called to someone inside the store.

"He's a-comin' again, Deke!" Then he stood there, smiling as though he alone had discovered something of momentous proportions.

Deke Spears stomped out of the store. He was a small man in his early thirties, and he made a practice of walking heavily so people would notice him. Spears had on an old pair of blue serge pants and a soiled apron, and, because the day was warm, he wore no shirt at all. There were holes and rents in his undershirt through which dense, dark hair protruded.

Three young boys and a long-haired dog

sprawled on the porch and Spears casually booted them into motion. "Git you some place else," he said, and thrust his hands into his pockets.

Two men came out of the store and stood there with Spears who listened to the car climb in low gear. Then he said: "I reckon the outlander's about to happen to an accident this time." He turned his head and watched the road, then the car came over the crown of the hill and started down, brakes protesting. The car was an old sedan that had been butchered and converted into a panel truck. As it came toward the settlement, other men took notice. The blacksmith left his forge and crossed to the store. Two other men left their shops and crossed the dirt street.

Jethro Langtry glanced at Deke Spears. "Be you goin' to cuss-fight him again, Deke?"

"I done that last time," Spears said. "This time I'll give him a hurt." He said no more for the car stopped by the porch and a man of fifty got out and flogged dust from his clothes. He wore a gray suit, a bit threadbare at the cuffs, and the warmth of the day had prompted him to loosen his tie.

He smiled and said: "From Louisville in nine hours." His glance settled on Jethro. "Have you moved from that spot since last month?"

The outlander was rather tall, grave-mannered, but not unsmiling. Although he was not frail, his shoulders were narrow and slightly rounded as though he had once shouldered many problems and had not quite completely recovered from the weight.

"From the jaw we had last month," Deke Spears said, "I reckoned I'd seen the last of you, peddler."

"I have a few promises to keep."

Spears frowned. "At the crossin' here, I'm boss. I sell everythin' from tools to baubees fer a pretty girl. There ain't nothin' you can offer folks hereabouts that I don't already sell. And I don't stand for no outlander cuttin' my prices." He pointed to the road beyond the settlement. "Go down that today, and you'll find it a sight harder to pass out than it was to go down it."

"Why are you afraid of me?" the outlander asked.

"Afraid?" Spears laughed. "What I got to be feared of?" He waved his hand to include all six buildings. "My pappy left all this to me. I have my say."

"Didn't the sheriff from Boonesboro hang your pappy, Mister Spears?"

" 'Peers strange you'd know of it," Spears said softly, cautiously.

"I heard it in talk."

He shook his head. "No, 'cause I don't 'low talk of it." He pointed to the car. "How come you keep the back locked up?"

"To keep your friends out of it when I'm inside having a cup of switchel," the outlander said.

Deke Spears suddenly clapped his hands together and turned to the blacksmith. "Anse, strikes me there's somethin' familiar 'bout him. Be you feel the same way?"

For a moment the blacksmith just stroked his whiskers, then he said: "Can't say one way or t'other. My recollect don't go far. Ain't like yours, Deke, what goes back plumb to the cradle."

Spears abandoned the blacksmith as a source of help. He spoke to the outlander. "Be your fore-parents from these parts? I swear you bring a recollect to me."

"No."

"I swear you're lyin' to me," Spears said. "I seen you before."

The outlander smiled. "Every time I've been here, you've seen me. That's my answer to your wondering."

It was the kind of an answer that would puzzle one man and amuse another; it puzzled Spears and amused the blacksmith. He left the porch, saying: "When the whuppin' starts, call me."

The outlander turned to his car and got in; the talk was ended and they all knew it. When he drove on out of the settlement and the dust finished blowing across the porch, Jethro Langtry said: "He ain't askeered of you none, Deke."

"I ain't put my hand on him yet," Spears said for the benefit of those listening, and went back inside his store.

• • •

The outlander drove slowly along the road; he had left Louisville before dawn just so he'd arrive at this afternoon hour, when the shadows were growing long through the trees and the woods held a piney flavor, a product of the heat and the dampness and an eon of undisturbed decay in the ground. He followed the narrow, rutted road for several miles, then turned off and drove across a small, grassy section of land to park in a grove of trees. He shut off the engine and got out of the car, then stood there, breathing deeply. The rotting remains of a low cabin was all but hidden by overgrowing brush, and he walked around it and stopped near an old stone pump casing. Across an interval of pasture he could see an old woman picking berries, but he did not attract her attention; he seemed content to be alone.

Finally the woman moved away, and the outlander waited as though making sure she was out of sight. Then he walked on past the well to the collapsed débris of an old barn. He hunkered down and studied the earth for a while. He packed and lit his pipe and his expression turned sad, as though he contemplated old troubles not completely gone from his mind.

Then he got up quickly and went back to his car, started it, and drove on down the road, which was forever winding and switching back. He slowed, rounded a tight bend, then came on the Drury place, and parked in the yard.

A woman in her early twenties was bending over a lye dip and near her boiled a cauldron of newly made soap. When he got out of the car, she smiled and waved, and, when he drew near, she said: "We've been expectin' you, far-travelin' man." She pointed to a hogback thick with timber. "Grams Drury ain't back from berry pickin'. Over to the Hobart place, I reckon."

"I saw her," the outlander said. "How be you, Marilee?"

She smiled because he lapsed into the vernacular of her people. "I be goodly, but sometimes work puts me on my bones." She dried her hands on the hem of her dress. "I'll bet you ain't et. Come in. There's some barefoot bread and I'll pour a cup of blue john for you."

He followed the lithe switch of her hips to the cabin, and, before he entered, he looked back at the hogback and saw the old woman with her basket of berries coming down the slope.

The outlander was sitting at the table when the old woman came in. She dumped her berries into a pail of water to keep them from spoiling.

"Hidy, far-travelin' man. Seen you at the Hobart place." She was a toothless bundle of bones, sixty years old, her skin a morass of wrinkles and folds. She reminded the outlander of some scarecrow in a milo field, garments hanging loosely

79

on the barest of skeletons. To Marilee, she said: "Get shet of your work before you talk. I'll speak with the far-travelin' man." She waited until the girl obediently left, then sat down at the table. "Brung you a baubee for Marilee this time?"

"Yes," the outlander said. "The dress I promised, and some earrings." Then he smiled. "And a shining frying pan for you, Grams."

The old woman snorted and waved her hand, but he knew she was pleased. "I got nothin' to pay with. Told you that before."

"A meal and a night's rest is enough," he said. "The Hobart place always had good berries. Too bad it just lays there, unworked. I wonder why Deke Spears hasn't grabbed it up. It don't belong to anyone."

Grams Drury looked steadily at him. "Funny you should say that. Deke's never gone near the place. He's been talkin'. Got it ag'in' you fer somethin'. It ain't like Deke to worry over a man. But he worries over you."

"It must be something from his past," the outlander said gently. "Something he's done and ain't been caught up with yet." He looked at her, and then laughed. "I never thought I'd fool you, Grams. You knew me right off and twenty years didn't make any difference, did it?"

"Twenty years ain't too long to recollect a night like that, or a killin'," she said. "Nobody 'round these parts has ever figured out what happened to Dawn Hobart. As fer the baby she had, they didn't know about that. I tended the birthin' and I don't say much." Her eyes pulled into wrinkled slits. "I knew you'd come back someday. And I waited fer it."

"Who knows me?"

"Ain't nobody knows you 'cept me an' the God who poured down the goose-drownedin' rain that terrible night." Her voice was scratchy, like an old Edison phonograph record he had once heard. "My own daughter had been sick abed with fallin' disease, and her carryin', too. The moment she died, there was a thunderclap and the sky let loose, like her goin' had shook somethin' loose up thar. I don't know which I grieved worse fer, her that was dead, or the child she took with her. I cussed God that night. Then you come to my door."

"The rain had stalled my car on the road," he said. "I was on my way to the Hobart place then, to get Dawn, to take her and the baby to Louisville with me." He raised his hand to his face and rubbed it. "What did she have to stay for? Her father was dead, murdered by Race Spears, and Race had been tried and hung on her testimony."

"You never once spoke out that she was your wife," Grams Drury said. "I never knew until you come to m'door. Far's I knew, the baby'd been born on the wrong side of the quilt."

81

"I was an outlander, a surveyor for the power company. Even her father was dead against me. We courted in secret, married in secret. Nothing we ever had saw the light of day." He shook his head. "It wasn't my way, to abide by mountain law and kill Race Spears because he'd killed her father. It wasn't my way of thinking, for the male survivor to seek revenge. I wanted it to end in a trial, not a feud. But how could I have known that Deke, an eleven-year-old boy, would murder her for revenge? How could I have known that, Grams?"

"You couldn't," she said. "You're an outlander. Deke warn't. He knew he ought to kill. It's the way of our people. But you've changed, outlander. You mean to have yer eye for an eye now?"

"Yes," he said softly. "I started to think of it the night of the rain, the night I found her in her bed, shot through. I held her as she died and she told me how the boy had broken in and fired without warning, then ran off, never knowin' there was the baby on the other side of the bed." He sighed. "Yes, I've changed. As I dug the graves beneath the manure pile and put your daughter beside my wife, I planned revenge. But I couldn't kill a boy. And I couldn't bring him to trial. I had to wait for the years to pass, Grams, the bitter, impatient years." He got up and refilled his cup with milk. "The first time I came back, I thought to have it out with him then, but I held back. The Hobart place was overgrown, rotted down. No one had never used it."

"There's a haunt to it, I hear tell." She shrugged. "Don't know how it got started. Deke's never gone near the place." She hesitated before asking her question. "Be you goin' to kill him, outlander?"

"I'm going to make him come to me," he said, "the way he came to Dawn, with the hate driving him and the bluster in him showing and the coward in him making his guts churn. It's a thing I live to see now, Grams."

"The past is all dead, 'cept your own flesh makin' soap out thar in the yard. The time's slipped by, between the night you fetched her across the hill in the rain, an' now. There ain't nothin' between but years."

The outlander got up.

She reached out and caught his arm. "Twenty years before, we didn't know yer name because we didn't give a mind to know."

"And now it doesn't matter," he said, "because my identity has long been lost. That man and this one are not the same." He stepped to the door. "I've got to go down the road a piece before it's full dark. I'll get your skillet from the car."

Both women went with him and waited while he unlocked the back door. Grams hugged the shiny skillet to her gaunt bosom, and Marilee

83

danced when she saw the dress and earrings.

The outlander got into the car and went on down the road. He stopped at the Harms place and gave them each something: a pair of shoes for the man, a set of Army surplus tin trays for the woman, and toys for the children. There was a shy young girl who hung back, and, before he drove out, he gave her a roll of well-eared movie magazines to make her dreams brighter.

As he traveled to the next place, he thought of his coming back, of that moment when he knew he would come back, but needed an excuse for being in the hill country. The notion of becoming a peddler came slowly, but it was a good notion. His funds were limited and he hadn't considered offering anything of real value. He'd bought a collection of matchbooks with bright covers depicting attractions from far places like Las Vegas and New York. He had intended on passing them out as a means of breaking the ice; they were all a stand-offish lot, but he hadn't counted on their reaction, which was delight and embarrassing gratitude. After they used the matches, they saved the covers and stuck them up on the walls. He had forgotten how they were, how narrow their lives were, and how much they never had. So he brought them little things, calendars by the score, a comb for a woman's hair, and a tie for a man who only owned one shirt.

Payment for these "baubees", as they called them, never entered the outlander's head. He'd eat a meal here and there, or sleep out the night in a shed or loft and bounced the children on his knee and to his ear would come the tales of trouble and disappointment and regret, and he always seemed to have a remedy for them, some half-forgotten bit of information to dredge up and offer. That they were helped at all was always a thing of amazement to him, for he could not escape the feeling of his own lack of worth.

He spent the night at the Kane place. Dal Kane was a pole of a man, slender to the point of emaciation. His wife was short and heavy and he had a brood of youngsters underfoot. Kane farmed ten acres and was considered a man well to do; he could afford to smoke a cigar now and then and owned a white shirt for Sunday wear.

"Cain't see what Deke's got ag'in' you," Dal Kane said. The children were in their ticks and he sat alone with the outlander while his wife strained milk on the back porch. "Cain't see where you mean a harm to Deke. 'Course, he's a hard man to figure. Wants his way. Gets his way, too." He glanced steadily at the outlander. "He's made his brag talk ag'in' you. He'll have to make it good or cut bait."

"I must remind him of something he dislikes."

Dal Kane stared for a moment. "Brings to my mind that he did say somethin' about you bein' a recollect of somethin'.'' Then he shook his head. "Deke's a strange one. Had his run of bad luck. First born to him was dead. He swore it was a curse put on him. The second was poorly in health. Didn't live a year. The third did, but it took his wife to the grave.''

"I didn't know he had a son," the outlander said.

"Yep," Kane said. "About six, come green up again."

"Did you ever wonder what happened to the Hobart girl?"

"Ain't nobody spoke of her fer years," Kane said, " 'ceptin' Grams Drury. But there's times when I see Marilee Drury and it comes to mind that Dawn held her head a certain way. But you shouldn't pay mind to all that Grams Drury says, outlander. Wouldn't surprise me none but what she started that talk about there bein' a haunt to the Hobart place. Some say at night you can hear a baby cryin'. 'Course, there's no truth to that."

"Have you been there at night?"

Dal Kane shook his head. "My business is here. Don't go around the Hobart place day or night. Nobody does, 'cept Grams Drury."

They talked of other things, then the outlander went to the loft to spend the night. He woke at dawn, went outside to wash, and had breakfast at Dal Kane's table.

He had two more stops to make, and it was mid-afternoon before he started back toward the village. As he passed some of the places, he noticed that the wagons were gone and that no one seemed at home. The reason for this wasn't clear to him until he got to the settlement and saw everyone there, just sitting around, waiting.

The outlander stopped his car and went into Deke Spears's store. A dozen men stood around, men he knew, men he had visited with only the day before, and they watched as he walked up to Deke Spears's counter.

"A cup of switchel," the outlander said, and laid a nickel on the counter.

Spears hesitated as though he wasn't sure whether or not to pour it. Then he filled a cup and shoved it toward the outlander. Jethro Langtry was standing away from the others, and he caught Deke Spears's eye, then went outside. While the outlander drank his switchel, Jethro took an iron bar and ripped off the padlock fastening the rear door of the panel truck. The outlander heard the rending of wood, but he paid no attention to it.

He said: "You won't find anything, Spears."

Jethro came back inside with a cardboard carton. "Ain't nothin' here, Deke, 'ceptin' some junk." He put it on the counter, and Spears pawed through it.

"Is that all you have?" Deke Spears asked.

"What did you expect me to have?" The outlander smiled.

Spears went out for a look, and came back with a .30-30 caliber rifle. He slammed this down on the counter and swore at Jethro for being blind. Then he whirled and faced the outlander. "What call you got to carry a gun?"

"Every man in this store has a gun," the outlander said.

Deke Spears shook his head. "They ain't outlanders!" He looked at each man standing there. "We got to protect ourselves."

"Against what? Outside of a few bear, what can hurt you here? Don't you live in peace? There ain't been a feud killing for twenty years. I hear there's a haunt near here. Do you need a gun to protect you from that?"

"I don't believe in any haunt," Spears declared.

"Why, I didn't know that," the outlander said pleasantly. "It was my understanding that you were the first one to hear the baby cry. Twenty years ago, wasn't it? In the rain, when you stood outside the Hobart place. You heard a baby crying then, didn't you?"

Deke Spears took an involuntary step backward. "I . . . I never heard no baby. I didn't hear nothin'!"

"Sure you did," the outlander said, taking a step toward him. "You was a youngster at the time, eleven or so. You remember because it was raining so hard and you'd just broken into the cabin and put a rifle ball into Dawn Hobart while she lay in bed. Then, because you were a kid, you got scared at what you'd done and ran, not noticing the baby. It was a natural thing. You didn't know she had a baby, and, if you had, it wouldn't have made any difference because kids don't notice what grown-ups are doing. But you heard the baby cry out, and you've never forgot it."

"Ah never did that!" He whirled and ran behind the counter and came up with a long-barreled pistol. "Ah'll kill you fer them lies!"

Dal Kane, who was standing near the end of the counter, opened his shirt and brought out a pistol of his own. Kane said: "When I left, I notioned I'd have need fer this today. We'll all hear what the far-travelin' man's got to say, so put the pistol down, Deke."

For a moment it was see-saw, then Spears lowered the gun. The outlander took his rifle from the counter top and held it in the crook of his arm. "I'm going outside, and I'll be there when you come out. You come with me to the Hobart place tonight, after dark, and I'll admit I accused you wrong."

"I don't go near that place," Spears said. "Ain't nobody else does, either!"

The outlander spoke to all the men there. "Who'll go with me tonight?"

Every man said that he'd go—except Deke Spears. The outlander had his answer, so he turned and walked out of the store and across the dusty street. He stood outside the blacksmith shop and faced the store. Some boys played on the porch with a long-haired dog and the street was quiet. Everyone waited patiently for Deke Spears to come out.

Finally the outlander spoke to a man near him. "Which young 'un is Spears's?"

The man pointed to a spindly-legged boy in faded overalls.

The outlander said: "Get him out of here. I don't want him to see this."

No one moved to send the boy away, and the outlander understood that this was their way. The boy would have to see the face of the man who killed his father, see it and remember it because the day would come when he'd have to face him, and the years wouldn't matter, just as they hadn't mattered to the outlander.

Deke Spears came out of the store then. He did not seem to be carrying a weapon. "I recollect you now, outlander. Twenty years ago you come into my pa's store and bought from him. Why? You ain't our kind. I did you no hurt."

"You took my heart," the outlander said. "You killed my wife."

It brought murmurs to their lips, complete understanding, complete sympathy, and Deke Spears heard them turn against him, drive him out like some diseased person.

"Ben, your name is!" Spears shouted. "Ben Travis! It's in Pa's old account books!"

"My name doesn't matter," the outlander said. "Spears, tell me why I shouldn't kill you now? Ask these people why I shouldn't take my rights, by your own laws, not mine?"

"I was a boy!" Spears shouted. "Just a boy!"

The outlander pointed to Spears's son who sat there full of bewilderment, scratching the dog's ears. "He's a boy. Six, seven maybe. Just old enough to remember my face. I'll be an old man when he comes for me. Sixty, anyway. What will I do, Spears? Will I stand there like you, with the coward in me for everyone to see? Or will I be lucky and kill him before he kills me?"

He shook his head and stood there for several minutes, trying to decide a question that only he understood. Then he took his rifle and smashed the barrel against the blacksmith's steel hitching rail, and smashed it again until it was forever ruined. Afterward, he threw it in the dirt and let his shoulders sag. "I've wasted my years, Spears. Wasted them waiting for you to grow into a man I could kill. A dozen jobs I've had and kept none of them because I knew someday I'd quit them to come back here. I've made nothing of my life. Nothing at all. Just wasted everything." An angry tone made his voice

91

strong and clear. "Go on, run your little store! Go on, live with yourself. And when it rains, toss in your bed and hear the baby crying."

This was his say, the sum total of his revenge, and it left him with nothing at all. He walked over to the car, and the people he had come to know went with him. When he started to open the door, Dal Kane put out his hand and held it closed.

"Be you no hurry to go some'ers," Kane said. "I'd be right proud to have you stay on a spell, far-travelin' man."

"You don't want him around here!" Spears shouted.

Kane ignored the man and the remark; he waited for his answer.

The outlander said: "My daughter lives here, Kane. Do you suppose . . . ? Yes, I'll stay a spell."

He got in the car and they all turned their backs on Deke Spears and got into their wagons and drove out of the settlement. Even Jethro Langtry deserted the store porch and went over to the blacksmith shop to do his standing and watching.

BELL'S STATION

I

Frank Bell had shed his youth twenty-five years ago when he took the Sharps rifle from his dead father's hands and fired at the Union troops storming their Missouri farmhouse. Whatever handsomeness youth had blessed him with had vanished as the wind and sun coarsened his angular features, dried his skin, and caused deep lines to form on a face that was only thirty-seven. His eyes were pale, far-seeing, old in the knowledge they held. If he had a thirst for beauty out on this great desert, that thirst remained unquenched, for there was nothing but the shimmering heat and the mountains to the north, perpetually veiled by distance. The land was monotony itself, plank-flat, unbroken to the four horizons.

Frank Bell had little, wanted even less. Behind the stage station that he managed lay three small outbuildings, a corral, a small blacksmith shop for emergency repairs, and nine hand-made crosses. Six were for the Mexican hostlers killed by raiding Mescaleros; the other three were in memory of a wife and two sons who fell to the same howling fury.

Three times weekly he faced the northeast, his hand shielding his eyes against the blazing sun, searching for the rising cloud of dust that would mark the coming stage. It was his break in a lonely land, a small pleasure taken for a few moments as these coaches touched him, then moved on. But now the coming stage carried a greater significance to him.

It was near noon and a bake-oven heat lay over the land. He had everything ready, the room, a few things he knew she would want. He had changed his clothes and combed his hair for the occasion. He was clean-shaven, except for the full mustache that nearly hid his mouth. He was like the land: gaunt, hard, with little about him that was excess.

He saw it then, a rising cloud as the driver tooled the swaying rig on the flats east of the Paradise. An hour later the red and yellow Concord was a large, bobbing dot, moving rapidly, dipping as it plunged through a dry wash, then coming into full view. He called to the Mexican boy who loitered by the barn and a fresh span, already harnessed, was led out to stamp impatiently before the low adobe station.

The stage was no more than a mile away now and he studied the plunging route it took, identifying the driver by the handling of the rig.

It took the last loop in the road, thundered through the arched gate, and skidded to a teetering halt before the door.

"Howlin' Mad" LongJake was handling the ribbons, his foot teetering on the brake. He glanced back at the smoking brake blocks, spat over the side, and said: "An hour and twenty-two from the Paradise, Frank. That's movin . . . ain't it?" LongJake was tall and wiry, with a high cheek-boned face that told people he was half Kaintuck and half Fox. He wore his hair braided, Indian fashion, and an assortment of deadly weapons hung from his belt.

Frank Bell pulled his eyes away from LongJake and looked into the coach. A drummer kicked the door open and dismounted to lean against a back wheel. A cattleman got out, giving LongJake a long, surly stare before turning to look out onto the flatness. Bell saw her then and moved forward to take her hand.

She was a tall woman with heavy bones, but she was pretty. Her eyes were blue and her hair fair; beyond that he didn't notice. He was a methodical man who believed there was a place for everything and now he turned from her, thinking of his passengers.

The Mexican hostler led the sweating team away and backed another in their place. Frank led the passengers into the station where LongJake announced: "Be a half hour. Feed up." He glanced at Bell and the woman, then went behind the bar and served the drummer and cattleman.

The woman swept the room with her eyes. Bell said: "You're Lilith Howard, aren't you?"

"Yes," she said in a smooth voice. "I'd like to clean up a little now." Her eyes met his squarely, like a man's might.

She was a little older than he'd imagined from her picture. She seemed a little more worldly than he would have liked, but he was a practical man and felt that he had no complaint. Heat lay heavily in the room, causing his shirt to stick to his back. He led the way down a narrow hall and indicated a room that was hardly more than a cubicle. She frowned, but said nothing and he turned away.

LongJake was talking in a loud voice when he entered the main room. He signaled for a Mexican boy to bring the food out, then went behind the bar as LongJake said: "The express office in Lordsburg was held up again, day before yesterday. Buck Wyatt was killed and another fella shot up bad. Elmer Sims done the shootin', but Dumb and Al was there. Nobody even tried to stop 'em when they left town."

"Why didn't you stop 'em?" Frank asked. "You say you was there."

LongJake shook his head and showed Bell the whites of his eyes. "Nosirree, this child ain't gonna do nothin' them Simses won't like!"

The drummer thumped his bowler and received another drink. He tossed it off nervously and said: "I heard that the marshal . . . Boomhauer . . . took after Elmer. Man's got guts, he has. Yessirree . . . real guts."

The cattleman raised his head and asked: "How's the Indians this year?"

"Still eatin' gove'mint beef," LongJake stated. "If I was runnin' the Army, I'd chase the hull lot of 'em down to Mexico." He swung his head to Bell and asked bluntly: "That your woman I brung in?"

"Yes," Frank said, but didn't add to it.

"Writ for her, didn't you?" LongJake shook his head sadly. "Damn sech company, anyhow. Tellin' a man this 'n' tellin' a man that. Had a squaw once myself. Crow gal . . . always talkin' . . . jabber, jabber, jabber. I ain't one for speech, this son ain't, and it like to drove me crazy. Traded her off to a Shoshone buck for a spotted pony and a jug of Joe Gideon tradin' whiskey. Fer all I know that gal might have that poor devil's ears talked plumb off by now."

The Mexican boy came in with the food and the drummer and cattleman turned to it as a welcome relief. LongJake stared at them for a moment, then turned his attention to his plate. Bell waited a moment, then went down the narrow hall and rapped lightly on Lilith's door.

"Just a minute," he heard her say, and the bolt

slid back. She wore a pale blue wrapper that outlined a full, mature figure. There was no shyness in her eyes when he looked at her.

Frank said: "I don't guess we know much about each other . . . Lilith."

"What's there to know," she said, "that ain't better guessed at?"

He nodded. "Be another stage in tomorrow . . . from Lordsburg. The preacher'll be on it to marry us, if you ain't changed your mind."

"I didn't come two thousand miles to change my mind. A woman my age ought to know what she wants." Her voice held no hint to her feelings, and, if she was disappointed, she didn't show it. She looked out of the small window and murmured: "Nothing, just nothing. Miles of it. Nothing to see . . . no place to go . . . nobody to talk to." She sighed and turned away.

There was nothing a man could say when a woman started to talk like that, Bell reflected. Clara had been like that toward the last. Never happy, always dreaming of something that didn't exist. Frank said: "I'll bring you a meal. You'll feel different about it after you been here a while."

She swung around to face him and again he sensed the wisdom in her eyes, that calm will behind her voice. "Will I?"

He went out because he had no answer, sending the boy in with a hot plate. He stayed in the main room, listening to the talk, then stood in the door as the passengers filed into the coach. LongJake mounted with a spry leap and gathered the reins between his fingers. "See you day after tomorrow," he said, and hit the brake with his foot. The coach surged, teetering on the heavy leather springs, and clattered from the yard, the wheels churning up a thick layer of dust.

He watched it for a moment, then turned as Lilith spoke by his elbow. "Good bye, people . . . good bye until next time." She leaned against the door frame, her full body relaxed, but it stirred him. She glanced at him, then turned and went on back inside. He said: "You're a mighty attractive woman . . . Lilith."

"How nice," she murmured, and a troubled line formed across his forehead. "I'm sorry," she added. "I had no right to act like that."

"Pays to be honest," he told her. "If you've changed your mind, you can go back."

She shook her head. "I don't have anything to go back to. Besides, I made a bargain. I always stick to my bargains, Frank."

He studied his work-hardened hands and said: "I was hoping it'd be more than a bargain. Man and woman gotta feel for each other to live out here. Gotta have something to hold 'em together."

"We'll see," she said, and went into her room.

There was no let up in the heat, but he had his work and it kept him busy until late afternoon.

She was waiting in the doorway as he came from the barn. "Damn this heat," she said. Her hair hung loosely around her shoulders. Sweat made a shine on her face.

"Cools off in the evening," he told her.

"If I live until evening." When he didn't answer, she went behind the bar and drew herself a glass of beer. She sipped it for a moment, then said: "You told me in a letter about a company rule. Only married men could run a place like this. Is that why you wanted to marry me?"

"They got a rule," Frank said. "That's a fact. I mentioned it 'cause I didn't want you to find out about it later and think what you're thinkin' now. I'm a lonely man. I thought I was writin' to another person like me . . . alone, needin' someone. I asked nothin' about you. I done that to show my faith. Maybe I should've asked."

"I haven't made a very good impression, have I?" She saw the answer on his face, but he was a kind man and wouldn't speak of it. She threw the rest of the beer away and added: "I don't know why I came here, either. I worked in a hotel for fifteen years . . . since I was thirteen. I always told myself that I'd get me a rich man and live some place where I didn't have to empty someone else's slops and wash their clothes. I don't like doin' for others! I want someone to do for me!"

He sat down at the table and clasped his hands. Her tone grated against him, but he pushed the hot words back and said instead: "This place is just a dirty little hunk of mud sittin' out in the middle of nowhere, but it's important. It's important to me and to a lot of people because it's safety where there ain't no safety. It's a holdover place for folks transferrin' to another stage. It's a meeting place in a wild land where places like that is scarce. It's a place where a man can find peace, just for a little while, or hell, if that's his inclination. I been here ten years. Ten years of heat and dirt and killin', but this is mine. *Mine!* I've poured my blood into it, and tears, and to me it's real . . . more real than any other place. I don't see much. I hear even less. I don't go no place, nor spend nothin', but I'm livin'. I don't have to run around the country lookin' for anything. It's right here. They come here and I see 'em and feel their troubles and hear 'em laugh. Sometimes it ain't pretty, what a man sees, but it's life . . . and Bell's Station is right in the middle of it."

She looked at him with that frankness in her eyes and said: "You're sure a windy cuss, ain't you?"

"I offered you something . . . a share in something dear to me. Maybe it ain't no good to anyone else, but it's good to me." The heat went out of him and he looked at the rough table top. "I'm sorry for you," he added, and fell silent.

• • •

Evening brought a welcome coolness to the land and Frank went around the room, lighting the lamps. Two of the Mexican boys were eating when Lilith came into the room. She looked at the rifles leaning against the table; the full bandoliers of cartridges draped across their chests, and asked: "Why all the guns?"

"Mescaleros," Frank told her. "They like to run off a few horses now and then . . . maybe lift a little hair if it's handy. Never hurts to be careful."

"This place makes me nervous," she said. "Mexicans with rifles. You with a pistol on your hip." She took a long breath and added: "Don't mind me. I'll get used to it. I'll have to."

"Person don't have to do anything," Frank said. " 'Course, he might have a few consequences to suffer through afterward, but that's beside the point."

"Don't sermonize me!" she said sharply. "Tomorrow, when that sin-killer gets here, we'll hold hands, then you'll be stuck with me and I'll be stuck with you."

"A poor way to put it," he muttered.

"You wanted a wife . . . I wanted a husband. You bought a blind pig . . . so did I. Let's not complain, shall we?" She didn't want him to answer her. "I'm going to bed," she told him, and went into her room. He heard her door close and the bolt slide shut.

He sat a long time in thought. . . .

102

II

Bell was up when the sun peeked over the horizon, but she didn't come out of her room until eleven. The heat was a strong thing, heavy and oppressive. He stood by the door, searching for the first glimpse of the stage, and she came out to stand beside him.

"What you watch like that for?" she asked. "It'll get here if you're watching or not. I saw you from the coach window yesterday . . . waiting, watching. What do you wait for?"

He couldn't explain it to her, what it meant to see that rising column of dust, that growing speck that meant life. He had lived with it too long, been too close to it for it to have clarity. He only knew that he needed it, found pleasure in searching for it. He touched her on the arm and pointed: "There! On the other side of the Paradise."

The rising plume of dust marked the stage, but there was no pause at the river, no halt to water the team. The coach dipped, sent a spray up and away, and lurched up the near bank, driving hard.

Frank's face mirrored a puzzlement. "The damn' fool! Is he trying to kill that span?"

He watched the coach leave the road and bounce across the flatness, the lathered horses at a dead run. He could make out the driver now, Monk Himmler, standing erect and lashing the team to a greater effort. Bell cursed and the Concord wheeled closer, then passed under the arch and came to a broad, sliding halt.

Monk took off his hat and mopped at the sweat streaming from his face. Frank's face was dark with temper as he said—"Damn you all to hell, Monk."—but Himmler cut him off with a sharp look and inclined his head toward the interior of the coach. Bell turned and jerked the door open.

The passengers made no attempt to get out, and he saw why. The man sat in the far corner; the others had moved away from him. One hand clutched a bullet-torn stomach, the other held a .45 Colt, rock steady. Across from him sat a man and woman. Her face was pale with fright and he chewed viciously on a cold cigar. Beside them, another man sat hunched over in the seat, nursing a hand with three fingers shot away. The preacher and two cattlemen made up the other passengers.

Bell looked at Elmer Sims and his torn hand and said: "You got yourself into it now, kid."

Sims was a young man, not yet twenty, but his eyes were wild and dangerous. His holster was empty, his clothes torn and dusty. He held his injured hand tightly against his chest. "You gotta help me, Frank." He spoke in a tight, windy whisper.

The man with the .45 moved his eyes, nothing

else. He spoke quietly but with authority: "Don't be a fool, Bell. I won't warn you again." He had a long angular face and pain had creased new lines in it, making runnels for dirt and sweat.

The coach rocked as Himmler swung down and shoved Bell aside. "It's your show, Marshal."

Boomhauer's voice was weak and full of pain. "I didn't expect this of you, Monk." He looked at the other passengers. "Everyone get out . . . except you, Sims. You stay."

The man and his wife hurried down, then she started to cry in a relieved way. The preacher uncoiled his length from the floor of the coach and stamped his feet to restore circulation. Neither of the cattlemen spoke—just went into the station for a drink.

Monk said: "You're hit bad, Charlie. You can't go on this way."

"I gotta," he said, but he knew Himmler spoke the truth. "All right . . . help me out, but don't get between this gun and him, understand?"

Bell and Himmler lifted him while Boomhauer bit his lips against the pain. They propped him, half erect, between them and he said: "Out, Sims. Behave or I'll kill you."

Elmer Sims got out and leaned against the wheel, still clutching his mutilated hand. He looked at the driver. "Monk! I never done nothin' to you . . . have I?" Himmler lowered his eyes and stared stonily at the ground by his feet. "Frank! Frank, you ain't forgot me, have you? You remember the time me 'n' Dumb come here when them Mescaleros was gonna storm the place! You ain't forgot, have you?"

"I ain't forgot," Bell said, and looked at Himmler.

"Found 'em on the road," Monk said. "Sims was carryin' the marshal on his back. Charlie had his gun barrel stuck right in Elmer's ear. They gotta have help, Frank."

"None of it here," Bell said, and a muscle flickered along the edge of his jaw when he looked at Boomhauer.

The marshal's head bobbed weakly, but the gun remained steady. It was as if he concentrated every bit of his strength on that gun, keeping it cocked and pointed at Elmer Sims. He said: "This man . . . my prisoner. I took him alive . . . I'll see him hang. I've warned you, Bell."

Sam and Himmler helped Boomhauer into the station. Lilith stood in the doorway, watching with eyes that were round with shock. Bell looked at her and shouted: "Get some hot water and clean clothes! Move!"

She came out of her fascinated state and ran toward the kitchen. The marshal objected when Bell wanted to put him in a room, so he spread blankets and a straw mattress in a corner. But first Bell sat him in a chair near the table, to make bandaging easier. At no time did that gun ever leave Elmer Sims.

Sims whined: "By God, Bell . . . what about me? This hand is bad!"

Frank looked at it and said bluntly: "You ain't got enough fingers there to pick your nose." He turned and stripped off the marshal's shirt.

The two cattlemen stood at the bar, their faces emotionless with only a small, detached interest in their eyes. The preacher sat at the table, his head bowed, speaking softly to an old friend no one could see. The man and his wife huddled against the far wall. She said in a loud whisper: "It's horrible . . . watching a man die like that."

"Shut up," her husband told her, and lighted a cigar with nervous fingers.

Boomhauer rolled his head toward Frank Bell and said: "I gotta get on that stage tomorrow. I may need some help."

"I'm not a lawman," Bell told him. "I don't want to get mixed up in this."

Lilith Howard came from the kitchen and set a bucket of hot water on the floor. Bell said— "This is gonna hurt, Marshal."—and cleansed the wound. Time passed with agonizing slowness and the room grew quiet as Bell worked. Boomhauer's face was drawn and white; whatever pain he felt he bore in stolid silence.

Bell glanced at Lilith and her mouth was pinched, her face shiny with sweat. He said: "Charlie, I can't get that bullet out."

Boomhauer didn't answer, except to nod

weakly. Bell helped him to the mattress and propped him up.

Himmler gave Elmer Sims a pint mug of whiskey and the man drank it hurriedly. He fastened his small eyes on Boomhauer and said: "I give you a good one, didn't I?" He laughed. "You can't eat. You can't drink. All you can do is lay there and leak blood. I'm laughin' . . . you understand . . . laughin'!"

The man's wife started to cry again and he spoke testily: "For God's sake, Marion!" The crying stopped and she moved away from him.

Monk Himmler banged his beer mug loud on the bar and announced: "All right, folks. Stage leaves in five minutes."

Boomhauer spoke: "No one leaves." He looked around the room at each of them, but particularly at the two cattlemen. "Elmer has friends. I can't handle them all. You all stay."

Monk Himmler swore. "Hell, Frank . . . he can't hold up a company coach!"

Bell looked at Boomhauer, and the gun he held. "He'll hold it," he murmured. He turned to Lilith Howard. "Better get some food on the table for these people."

"Is that an order?" she demanded.

"No," Bell said with deliberate slowness. "That's courtesy." He saw color rise in Lilith Howard's face and she turned and went into the hot kitchen.

Frank went behind the bar and drew himself a beer. One of the cattlemen nodded toward Boomhauer and asked: "Think he'll last?"

Bell shrugged. "He's got a will. Hard to say about a man like that."

The cattleman's face pulled smooth and he murmured: "Yeah. I guess it is at that." He gave his friend a sidelong glance, then fell silent.

Sims sat on the floor, not more than ten feet from the marshal. He wore a bandage around his hand now, but he paid it scant attention. He never took his eyes from the marshal's gun. Bell watched him for a long moment, then whispered: "I've seen Elmer and his brothers a dozen times when they stopped here, but I never seen him like that. He's more animal than man." He finished his beer quickly and washed the glass.

The preacher left the table and touched Bell on the arm. He gave the marshal a troubled glance and said: "Ah . . . when do you want the ceremony to take place?"

"Ceremony?" Bell remembered then. "Later . . . tomorrow, maybe."

"I don't know now," the preacher said. "I have to get back to Lordsburg." He gave Boomhauer another glance and said: "All right . . . all right."

The afternoon wore on. The coach sat alone before the station and the Mexican boys found pressing chores around the barn and corral. The main room was stifling with the heat of a dying sun. Boomhauer remained on his pallet of straw, head dropped forward, but everyone sensed his awareness. To Bell, it was as if he were saving a small unit of his strength, waiting for the break he knew would come, to let it burst forth then, and snuff out as life fled from him. He was the weakest, most helpless, but by far the most dominant; he was stronger, somehow, than any other.

Elmer Sims had not moved. He still huddled on the floor, saying nothing, only moaning softly occasionally.

The man and his wife remained at the table, and her face was pale and drawn; he smoked one cigar after another and drank more than was good for him. The two cattlemen remained stonily silent. Even the preacher seemed to have lost his taste for prayer.

Lilith stood in the archway, leading into the kitchen, and Bell took her arm, moving to the rear of the adobe. He said: "He can't last this way. God only knows what's keeping him alive with that bullet in him. I never seen anything like it in my born days."

"You could take that man away and tie him up." She saw his face settle, and added: "But you don't want to, do you?"

"No," Frank admitted. "Everyone stops here,

Lilith . . . the good and bad alike. The Sims brothers have been welcome here and Boomhauer knows it. Al and Dumb got into a shooting scrape a while back and Boomhauer came here after them. I refused to let him take them. I didn't want any shooting. He wouldn't trust me now. I don't blame him much."

"You're afraid of them," she said bluntly. "You're thinking of the other two and what they'd do if you turned on Elmer."

"We'd better get back out there," Frank said tonelessly, and led the way down the hall.

The man—his name was Meeker, he'd said—stood next to his wife, but it was habit, not affection that drew them close. He was a blunt-faced man with a full, roan mustache and quick, dark eyes. He wore a dark suit and his hat sat squarely on his head. Lilith glanced at them, then touched him. "Perhaps your wife would like to lie down for a while."

The severity on the man's face vanished and he swept off his hat, displaying hair that was wavy and damp. This gallantry had been unexpected and Lilith glanced at the small woman in time to catch the sudden hurt in her eyes. Meeker caught this, too, and, realizing his unconscious error, put his hat back on, and studied the land through the window with a pointed concentration. Lilith led the woman away, and a moment later Bell heard her weeping deep in the rear of the station.

Frank looked at Meeker, but the man found the ash on his cigar fascinating. Bell nodded toward Boomhauer and asked: "Why the hell don't you help him?"

"Not my concern," Meeker said in a soft voice. "I don't want that Sims tribe after me." He raised his head quickly and gave Bell a long look. "Help him yourself. This is your station." He turned to the bar and poured himself another drink. Bell went over and took the bottle away from him. Meeker's eyes got stubborn and a little mean. He said: "What's the matter, Bell? You think I can't afford to pay for it?"

"You've had enough," Frank stated. "I don't want a drunk on my hands, too." Meeker's mouth twitched and he swayed forward, but gave it up and went back to the table to sit.

Frank crossed to Boomhauer's corner and asked softly: "Anything I can do for you, Charlie?"

The marshal raised his head slowly, as if the effort cost him more than he could afford. Although his face was ashen and his eyes sunken, he still clung to a certain handsomeness. He nodded. "Find me a friend, Bell. I'm going out pretty soon."

"Take your pick," Frank said, and Boomhauer looked at each of them. Monk Himmler stared back at him for a moment, then his eyes wavered and he turned back to the bar. The two cattlemen showed only a stiff-faced neutrality, but they were uneasy and couldn't hold his eyes. The preacher never raised his head. Meeker dropped his eyes and stared at a knot on the rough table top. Elmer Sims saw this and knew how it was. He grinned hugely at the marshal and nursed his crippled hand.

The calm fatalism in Boomhauer was reflected in his voice. "It don't make much difference. Man don't have friends when he packs a star. He won't get far. Someone else will get him."

Bell's lips pulled into a thin line and he hurried into the back room. He said to Lilith: "Better start another meal. The Mexican boys won't come near the house as long as Sims is in here."

"All right," she said, then added quickly: "He's gonna die . . . isn't he?"

"He knows it," Bell said savagely. "Dammit, he knows it and he just sits there like a god . . . right and, somehow . . . holy."

She looked at him for a drawn moment, then murmured: "You're fighting yourself, Frank. You know what's right . . . then do it."

"I wonder what the others have against him?" Curiosity was nibbling at him and he went back to the main room. Meeker had been into the bottle again and his eyes were getting red-rimmed. He sat alone at the table, sunk in his own thoughts when Bell sat down across from him. Bell said softly: "He's dying, Meeker."

"Let him die, then," Meeker said with a coldness that didn't quite come off. He glanced at Boomhauer and the effect was startling. Meeker's eyes misted and he dropped his head, staring at his clenched hands. The whiskey had loosened him, allowing his feelings to slip up on him. He spoke with a soft viciousness. "He sits there . . . like nothin' could move him. He makes a man feel small, like dirt, when he wants to. I don't like for no man to make me feel like dirt."

"Boomhauer never struck me as that kind," Bell stated flatly. "You got a guilty conscience?"

Meeker scrubbed his face with his hand. At another time he would have been fighting mad, but now he was feeling mellow and faintly regretful. "We don't get along any more . . . Marion and me. A man's a fool when his woman don't love him." He gave Bell a dark glance and added: "Boomhauer's right . . . I'm no good. There was a woman in Lordsburg, not too good a woman. He knew what I was up to and run her out of town. It'd been better if he'd told it around. Somehow I just can't bring myself to thank him for it."

"You're acting like a jackass about it," Bell opined. Meeker made no reply, just touched a match to his dead cigar and sat, deep in thought.

Elmer Sims shifted on the floor and Boomhauer came alert. He pointed the muzzle of his .45 at the man, and Sims grew quiet. Bell watched this and understood what Sims was doing. Every move cost the marshal some of his remaining strength, brought him that much closer to the end. Sims was playing a wicked game. Bell knew it when he saw the film of sweat appear on Boomhauer's face.

Bell went to the bar to clean the glasses and stack the bottles. The cattlemen leaned heavily and one of them beckoned with a curled finger. "How's he doin'?" He was a big man, blunted by the land and his face was intolerant of anything outside the sphere of his own thoughts.

"Dyin'," Bell said, and watched for a flicker of emotion.

The tall cattleman looked at his friend and something passed between them and was gone. "He's alone," the man said. "I always wanted to see him with his back against the wall, but damned if I take any pleasure in it now."

His friend studied his hands and murmured: "It ain't right, Chess . . . us doin' nothin' like this."

"Shut up!" The big man spoke sharply. "No man hits me and then makes me forget it!"

"You was drunk, Chess," the other man said. "He was doin' his job, that's all." Chess had folded his hands and was studying the surface of the bar bracketed by his forearms. The other man closed his mouth and stared out onto the land.

Chess said: "A man hates to admit he's a fool. I made some strong talk to him some time ago." He looked at Bell with a large question in his eyes and asked: "How can he stay alive? What's holdin' him up?"

"He's better than you or me," Bell said. "We ain't nothin' compared to him."

The preacher sat, unmoving, until Bell touched him on the shoulder, then he raised his head, impatient at this interruption. "It's blasphemy," the preacher said tonelessly. "He's dying and yet he ignores God."

"Maybe he knows more about God than you do," Bell said. "What's holding him up if it ain't God?"

"I offered to pray for him in the coach," the preacher said as if he hadn't heard Bell. "He told me to get out of the way . . . to pray for the other man because he needed it worse. He told me not to get between them or he'd shoot right through me."

Bell stood up, feeling a small anger rising against the man. "You'd better turn that collar back around, Preacher. You ain't any better than the rest of us."

Lilith came out of the kitchen and began putting food on the table. "I fixed him some broth," she said. "Do you think he can drink it?"

He nodded and took it from her. Boomhauer was slow to answer his touch. He looked at the

116

broth as if he couldn't see it, then murmured: "Why, Frank? The last time . . . you told me to go to hell."

"That was the last time," Bell said, and gave it to him a little at a time. He took it all, then leaned back and nodded his thanks. Bell noticed that he was bleeding again. The bandage he had put around him was beginning to soak through.

Boomhauer took the man by the sleeve and pulled him close: "Bell, I made a mistake. Let the coach go. Al and Dumb will know I got Elmer. I don't want them killin' anyone here."

Bell looked at him, trying to see behind that pokerface, but gave it up. "They'll shoot you to rag dolls when they get here," Frank said, but Boomhauer had lowered his chin to his chest again and acted like he hadn't heard. Bell rose and crossed to Monk Himmler. "Load up. Send back some help from Tombstone."

Monk looked at the marshal and said: "I'll do that much for him." He turned away, but Bell pulled him back, holding him with a grip on the sleeve.

"What's eating you?"

"Nothin'," Monk stated with a mild stubbornness. "I been on the dodge myself. I feel for anyone runnin' from a badge." He let his voice boom in the room. "Stage leaves in fifteen minutes. Better get outside, them that's goin'!"

The two cattlemen looked at each other, but

remained rooted. The preacher raised his head, half rose from his seat, then relaxed. Meeker gave Monk Himmler a long study, then went back to his cigar.

"You wanna get yourself killed?" Monk asked. Faces tightened; a frown appeared on the preacher's face, but no one answered. Monk said—*"Agh!"*—and went outside.

Lilith came to the archway and motioned for Bell. She asked: "Is he better?"

"Who knows?"

"It's a shame he has to die," she whispered. "What a waste."

A thought circulated through Frank Bell's mind. He understood the cattlemen and why they stayed. Neither wanted the other to think he was eager to leave; it was a matter of pride with them. The preacher wouldn't leave alone. He'd remember that and never be the same again. Meeker was full of trouble and whiskey, confused, uncertain. Bell said suddenly: "There's three rifles and a carton of shells in my closet. Bring them out and lay them on the bar, will you?"

"What . . . ?"

He took her shoulders and turned her. "Just bring them out." He went back to the main room to wait. Outside, Himmler fought the span alone. His cursing filtered back into the building and harness buckles jingled as he fastened the traces. The cattlemen remained rooted in moody silence. Bell spoke to them. "There'll be gun play when Sims's brothers get here."

"I've heard shootin' before," Chess stated.

Bell nodded and turned away.

III

Lilith had his rifles laid out on the bed when he came into the room. He said: "How's Missus Meeker?

Lilith shrugged. "How does a woman feel when her husband no longer loves her?"

"I guess they're both mixed up," Bell said. "I guess we all are. I know you don't like it here, but it was kind of you to fix him broth and such . . . real kind."

"Last night I hated it," she said. "I cried, feelin' sorry for myself." Suddenly she buried her face in her hands and murmured: "I'm wicked . . . wicked. I've been hoping he'd die. Die so the other man would go because I don't want a man bleeding on my floor. God forgive me!"

"I always wondered what I saw in Boomhauer's face," Frank said. "It was loneliness. He has no one and he's alone now, dyin' alone, without sympathy, without help, without anything." He sighed and picked up the rifles. She carried the ammunition and laid it beside the rifles on the bar. Bell stood back and waited.

Chess looked at the .44 Winchester as if he had never seen one before. He glanced at his friend, then said: "A man lives longest when he keeps his nose outta other people's business." He glanced out the open door at the waiting stage. "There it sits. All a man'd have to do is git on and it'd all be behind him. Man's a fool to interfere," he added, and picked up a rifle, loaded it, and tucked it under his arm.

The preacher raised his head at this soft disturbance, then rose and crossed to the bar. He touched one of the rifles and said: "This is the tool of the devil. Is there no righteousness in this godless country?"

Chess turned to him. "Make your own, Parson. There's shells aplenty and a window to shoot out of."

"I've never killed a man," the preacher said softly, as if he were trying to tell himself something.

Chess looked at him and jerked a thumb toward Elmer Sims. "You think he's a man?"

The preacher lifted the gun and fumbled as he fed cartridges into the loading chamber.

Meeker said: "I want to see my wife." Bell motioned toward a back room and the man hurried as if a great urgency pressed against him. Lilith Howard watched this and understood what Bell had done. He crossed to the door and looked out upon the land.

Monk Himmler was waiting by the coach. He said: "One minute left, Bell. Any of them coming?"

Frank shook his head.

Himmler spat into the dust and murmured— "It's a lonely ride by myself."—and took his Spencer from the boot, shouldering past Bell to go inside. Frank closed the door and slid the bolt.

Sims was still crouched on the floor, letting his wild eyes wander around the room. He knew what was going on and he grew nervous. He looked at Chess and said: "You don't know what it's gonna be like. You'll get it good for this . . . slow . . . like he got it."

"Shut your mouth," Bell said flatly.

Sims flipped his head. "I'll remember you. We come through here plenty. You was our friend then. Dumb'll take care of you, Bell."

Light began to fail outside and Lilith lighted the wall lamps. There was no sound, save Boomhauer's ragged breathing. Meeker and his wife came into the room and Bell saw that he had told her what she wanted to hear. Somehow this pleased him.

The cattlemen moved to the two front windows. Chess cradled the rifle; the other man held a Colt in his right hand, another thrust in the waistband of his trousers. The preacher was in the kitchen, sitting in the dark to shoot a man.

Monk took his Spencer and went to Bell's room that faced the corral and outbuildings.

Frank spoke to Lilith. "There's a trap door in the kitchen leading to the root cellar. Take Missus Meeker and go down there."

She produced a long-barreled Smith and Wesson from the folds of her apron. "This is my house, too," she said. "I wouldn't run from the devil himself."

Meeker and his wife stayed by the wall. He held Bell's rifle across his knees. When he spoke, it was to no one in particular. "Funny thing about a man. He'll go along, thinkin' he's somebody, and all the time he's nothin'. He does things he shouldn't, hides it, then finds out he's been a damn' fool."

"A man who can admit that is no fool," Bell told him.

Chess got up and paced nervously. "This waitin' is hell," he said.

Meeker pointed to Sims and said: "What about him? What happens to him when his brothers get here?"

"I hadn't thought about it," Frank admitted. He hated to take the man away from the marshal.

Sims said: "You better not hurt me! You better watch yourselves. You think them Mescaleros is mean . . . you just wait. You'll see!"

"Boomhauer's right," Chess said, and turned, pointing the rifle at Elmer Sims's head. "Stand up!" he ordered. "Stand up, damn you!" Boomhauer heard the call and tried to raise his head. His gun still pointed at Sims, the focal point of his remaining strength.

The cattleman raised the rifle quickly and the room thundered as he triggered it off, working the lever even as the report hung—slamming a fresh shell into the chamber. Elmer Sims screamed and clasped a hand to his head. Blood poured from between his fingers where Chess had shot the lobe off of his ear. The cattleman's voice was low and deadly: "Git up off that floor . . . you killin' savage!"

Sims didn't waste any more time getting to his feet. The other man toed a chair around, and Meeker went in back for a rope. Sims didn't fight when they bound him because Chess pressed the muzzle of the Winchester between his eyes and said softly: "One squeak . . . one little move, and I'll blow the head right off of you!"

Boomhauer watched this with dulled eyes, then his head flopped forward and the gun slipped to the floor. Lilith cried out and ran to him. Mrs. Meeker left her husband's side and together they laid him flat.

Lilith was saying: "He's still alive, Frank . . . still alive!"

"We'll keep him that way," Bell said with a great deal of confidence that he hadn't realized he had.

Chess had thrown a rope over one of the cross beams in the ceiling and opened the front door. There was no talk, yet each man understood what was going on. Chess said: "Meeker, can you tie a hangman's knot?"

Meeker shook his head.

"I can," the other man said, and Meeker tossed him the rope.

"Make a good knot, Harry," Chess told him, and Harry wove thirteen coils into the lariat.

Elmer Sims's face was pale and frightened.

"No! No, please! You wouldn't do that!"

Chess pointed the rifle between Sims's eyes and ordered: "Mount up!"

Sims got on the chair. Meeker draped the rope over his neck and fastened it to the far wall. Harry helped him pull it tightly enough to cut off a little of Sims's wind. Lamplight streamed out of the open door and Meeker said: "All right, Sims, we'll wait for your brothers. When they get here and start shooting, we'll kick that chair out from under you or fall across the rope. There won't be any bullet for you, Sims . . . just a rope, like the marshal wanted it."

At nine o'clock Lilith went into the kitchen to make coffee. Frank waited until the others were served, then joined her. She looked tired, but some of the discontent had vanished from around her mouth. They sat at the small table with only a solitary lamp for light and talked. He told her of his dead wife and sons. He talked of the land as a man will who has lived his life in it, sincerely, with no apology for it.

Boomhauer had been moved to Bell's room and was resting. Mrs. Meeker had packed the wound with flour to stop the bleeding, and it had been an hour since any flecks of blood appeared on the marshal's lips. Bell thought of this and said: "Maybe he's stopped bleeding inside. They sometimes do that."

The preacher turned and spoke from the shadow-draped corner that was his post. "God is with that man." Bell looked at him for a long time, then smiled, and the preacher turned back to study the land.

It was after twelve when Harry came into the room and Bell blew out the lamp before going into the main room. He asked Chess: "Hear someone out there?"

"Horses," he stated. "Quiet now, though."

"Blow out all of the lamps," Frank ordered. "Leave that one on the far wall to show the boys up here." Meeker moved around the room, cupping his hand over the glass chimneys. Soon there was only one lamp remaining.

Chess said: "I can go out there and take a look around."

"You can get shot, too," Bell told him. "Stay

put. If they want him, then they'll come in and get him."

The silence grew long and each man breathed through an open mouth, straining to catch the slightest sound. Out near the corral a horse snorted nervously. In front, by the door, the coach reared up, dark and heavy-looking. The team was still in harness, but standing three-legged and patiently. Beyond the coach, a shadow rose and shifted, then a rough voice called out: "Boomhauer! We know you got him! Let him go!"

Bell cupped his hands around his mouth and yelled: "Come on in, but keep your guns outta your hands! We got him standin' on a chair with a rope around his neck. Start trouble and we'll hang him!"

"That was Dumb," Harry supplied. "I know the voice."

"Friend of yours?" Bell asked.

Harry looked sheepish and sidled a glance at Chess. "Not exactly, but he's worked for me off and on."

"Dumb!" Bell called out. "Come on in and see before you start anything!"

"Is that you, Bell?" the man called. "What's the matter, Bell? Whose side you on anyhow?"

"Come in and find out!"

"No tricks now!" Dumb called, then a shadow rose and moved toward the door with a slow-witted caution.

The small lamp left the room in near darkness, yet he stared at the light and blinked. He took a step toward his brother, but Chess threw up the rifle, and he halted. He was a giant with large hands and arms that dangled loosely. He had the quick, glassy eyes of the mentally retarded. He watched Frank Bell with a naked hatred. "You was our frien'," he said. "You let us stop here. Now you got poor Elmer with a rope around his neck."

"You saw him, now get out of here," Bell said. "Take Al with you."

Dumb didn't understand it. "Why you doin' this, Bell . . . and the rest of you fellas . . . why?"

"We're doin' this for a friend," Chess said. "A friend who'd do the same for us."

"We'll get you for this," Dumb said. "Al's out by the well. We'll cut off your water. We'll burn you out like the 'Paches."

There was that great, stupid determination about the man that filled Frank Bell with sudden warning. He glanced at Chess and knew that he'd caught it, too. Chess moved closer to the chair and Harry drew the other gun from his waistband, cocking both of them. Bell repeated: "Get going, Dumb. There's nothing you can do."

Dumb's heavy face settled and he turned away, but Bell dropped his hand to his gun, drawing it as the big man wheeled back around. Chess swung the rifle like a club, sending the chair kiting. The rope sang as it took the sudden weight. Dumb had his gun out and working. Harry and Frank Bell shot together. The man stumbled back, but retained his gun, somehow managing to stay on his feet. He shot again, blindly, then strength fled from him, and he fell like a big tree, solid and earth-shaking.

Mrs. Meeker hid her face in her hands and Lilith moaned softly. Out in back a shout went up, then silence fell. Harry said in a tight voice: "That's Al."

Frank Bell mopped his mouth and muttered: "I'll go. I don't want any more shooting in here with the women."

Meeker stepped away from the wall. "Al introduced me to a woman in Lordsburg once. I always wanted to pay him back." Meeker turned to his wife and she smiled. He kissed her, then stepped out the door. Frank Bell followed him.

The Mexicans had barricaded themselves in the barn. Bell touched Meeker and pointed to the harness shed next to the corral. A man moved out there; a horse snorted and jumped away. Monk let one go from his .56 Spencer and Al Sims left the building, running, bent over, across the backyard. Meeker raised his gun, but Bell took his arm again and shook his head.

He led the way, ducking around the building corner, then stopping with the front door on their right and not more than fifteen feet away. They waited for what seemed a long time, then a shadow detached itself from the wall and moved slowly toward the open door. Bell's hands began to sweat and he wished he'd thought to cock his gun, but it was too late now.

Al Sims's boot toe touched the edge of the light and clothing rustled softly as Meeker raised the rifle to his shoulder. Sims stood there, wrapped in blackness, looking at Dumb who lay sprawled across the sill. He stepped into the light suddenly, a gun in each hand, and Bell yelled—"Wrong way!"—and fanned the hammer.

Meeker's Winchester belched fire as Al wheeled, shooting. Meeker cursed and dropped the rifle even as his bullet slammed into the slat-thin gunman.

Al staggered against the frame, bracing himself. Bell shot again, low, catching him in the stomach. Al had dropped one of his guns when Meeker's bullet tore through his chest. Now he fired the other one blindly into the dirt at his feet as he crumpled.

Lilith re-lighted the lamps. The Mexicans ventured to the corner of the station and crossed themselves. Meeker sat in a chair while his wife removed his coat and bandaged his upper arm where Al's bullet had stripped away a long hunk of meat. Harry and Chess came out and toed the dead man over. Chess spat into the dirt and said: "Good riddance."

Monk and the preacher emerged from the rear of the house. Monk went to the bar and poured himself a generous drink. The two cattlemen cut Elmer Sims down, then carried him to the barn. They made two more trips after Dumb and Al.

Lilith fixed another pot of coffee and the men slumped in their chairs, saying nothing, but thinking a lot. Bell went to see Boomhauer who lay, pale and drawn, against the dark blankets. He was awake. Bell leaned forward to hear him. "I heard shooting."

"Al and Dumb Sims," Frank said. "They're dead."

"Elmer?"

"Hanged," Bell said. "Just like you wanted it."

It pleased Boomhauer because he closed his eyes and a tight smile creased the corners of his lips.

Monk Himmler had lighted the coach lamps and was making up for his run. Meeker went outside with his wife. The two cattlemen and the preacher were already in the coach. Bell said: "We'll come in to town this week-end, Reverend. That all right?" The man nodded, and Bell stood back.

Meeker turned to him and said in a half-joking voice: "I think I'll complain about the service. I never seen a time when it took so long to get from one place to another."

The coach lanterns cast an eerie light onto the

ground and the horses moved impatiently. Bell looked at him for a long moment and said: "Sometimes it takes a man a long time to get where he's goin'." Meeker nodded at that and took his wife's arm, helping her into the coach.

Monk sat on his high perch, looking around him. "I've been here a hundred times, but this is the first time I ever noticed the damn' place."

He kicked his foot off of the brake and shouted the team against the harness. Bell stood and watched it lurch off into the night, lights bobbing as it cut onto the road and picked up speed. Only the soft voices of the hostlers broke the quiet.

Lilith Howard was waiting when he went inside and he paused in the doorway to look at her. She was the same woman, tall with a full, flaring body, but Bell sensed a difference, a mellowness that she had not possessed before. "How's the marshal?" he asked.

"Better," she said. "I got some hot coffee down him and a little more broth."

He pursed his lips and nodded, looking out onto the land. It was cool now, with a gentle breeze blowing from the northeast, but tomorrow the sun would come and with it more heat. He heard Lilith's movement behind him, then she lay her head against his arm and said: "I've a big washing tomorrow. I hope it's hot as blazes."

She grew quiet for a moment and he said nothing, feeling that she was reaching for something, something she needed. He had no wish to spoil it.

"It's a beautiful land, Frank . . . so quiet. Tomorrow another coach will come. I think I like the world coming to my front door."

He looked at her and saw that she was smiling.

WILDCAT ON THE PROD

I

It was dusk when they topped the hill overlooking Wineglass, pausing to rest their horses before making the last winding dash off of the slope and into the town. Lamplight streamed from the shop windows in pale streaks, and riders pounded into town, pulling into the tie rails that lined each side of Custer Street.

Bert Kerry glanced at his friend and shoved his best hat to the back of his head. He took a cigar from the breast pocket of his suit coat and licked it into shape, one leg hooked around the saddle horn. "Sure is pretty this time of night, ain't it?"

The other man shot him a quick, half-believing glance and murmured: "Just gotta pull the lion's tail, don't you?" He was tall in the saddle and wire-thin with almost no waist. His cheeks were long and sunken, and his blond hair was bleached white against the darkness of his skin.

"Hell," Bert said, "I was robbed the last time, and you know it . . . gangin' up on a fella that way."

"I don't see why," Bob Overmile said. "We gotta ride sixty miles just so you can spark a gal and get your face slapped for stealin' a kiss. We plumb wore out our welcome in this here town."

Kerry raised his head quickly, giving his friend a very pained look. He was short and stocky with a flat face that was anything but pretty, but there was something compelling in his eyes and humor lurked around the edges of his mouth. He glanced at the peaceful town and said: "They don't understand us, that's all. They got off on the wrong foot with us the last time. I want to give 'em all another chance. Every man gets a second chance, that's my motto."

"Motto, hell," Bob said. "You want to see Milo and pick a fight." He lifted the reins, indicating that he was impatient to be under way. Kerry snuffed out his smoke, and then there was no more talk. Fifteen minutes later they crossed the covered bridge north of town and traveled the length of Custer Street.

They pulled in at the hitch rack before Murphy's Hotel and dismounted. Frank Burk, the marshal of Wineglass, had been taking his ease with his feet elevated on the porch railing. These now hit the floor with a *thump,* and he rose and crossed to the edge of the boardwalk. He was a big man, tough-faced, but there was no meanness in his eyes when he spoke. "Well . . . Kerry! You must have liked our jail."

Bert shot him a quick smile and said: "You could have gone all night without sayin' that." He turned his head and looked up and down the street.

"No need to look," Burk said in a half-joking voice. "We got all the women locked up until you leave town."

"Hell," Bert said, "I thought there was a dance tonight at the schoolhouse."

The marshal lighted a cigar and spoke around it. "There is, but I gotta warn you . . . any trouble and into the cooler you go." He gave Bob Overmile a quick look and added: "That applies to you too, Overmile. I remember you from the last time." He made a turn as if to leave, then held out his hand. "I almost forgot . . . I'll take your guns."

"What the devil!" Bert said, then saw the determination in the marshal's face, and reached under his coat for his .38-40. Bob Overmile produced a short-barreled Colt, and Frank Burk said: "If you boys can stay out of trouble, you can have these when you're ready to leave town. I'll have 'em over at the jail."

"I don't want to go near the place," Kerry said with mock seriousness. "You can lay 'em on the boardwalk." The marshal grinned and went back to his chair on the verandah. Bert Kerry stretched and rubbed his stomach, then said: "A drink at Garfinkle's and then a night of gaiety."

Bob Overmile slanted him an unbelieving glance, and they cut across to the saloon. Garfinkle had a fair crowd at this early hour; the piano player rendered a fast tune with more industry than talent, but the customers made no objections, even applauded vigorously when he finished. Bert found a place near the end of the bar and caught Garfinkle's eye. The saloonkeeper paused and glanced around him as if he were taking a rapid inventory of the breakable items, then slid along the length of the bar, and stopped before them. "No trouble tonight, fellas," he said. "Milo don't want no trouble, either."

"I'll bet he don't," Bert said, and ordered two beers. He reached a stout arm across the bar and took a firm but friendly grip on Garfinkle's string tie. He pulled the man close and said: "Mary ain't married that son-of-a-sheepman, has she?"

Garfinkle's eyes grew round with shock. He looked around hastily as if fearful someone had heard the remark. "My God," he said, "what a thing to say about a Texan! No, she ain't married him and never will. Somehow, she thinks he's short weight."

"He is," Bert stated, "and I'm gonna show her how short before I get older."

Garfinkle let out a long breath and tapped his head with his forefinger. Overmile's grin said that he agreed with this. The saloonkeeper took

Kerry's sleeve and said: "You're a good fella, Bert. You don't drink too much, you got a good job, and you save your money, but you're too stubborn. You don't believe a man when he says no, and, when he swats you, you think it was a lucky punch. Be a good fella and go back to Hondo. Don't grab the tiger by the tail tonight."

"Why?" Bert wanted to know.

Garfinkle rolled his eyes until they showed a large expanse of the white, and said: "Milo Weeks and some of the young bucks got their heads together and decided to rough you up a little bit if you went near the schoolmarm. I ain't sayin' Mary likes the idea, but there ain't much she can do about it without makin' a damn' fool outta you. Play it smart and don't go near that dance tonight."

"That's what I come here for," Bert said.

"I give up," Garfinkle admitted. He looked at Bob Overmile, who viewed the whole conversation with a great deal of tolerance, and said: "Can't you do anything with him?"

"Nobody can," Overmile said. "Just let him run and someday he'll hit something he can't lick, and it'll either cure him or kill him."

Bert drained his beer and said to Overmile: "Stick around for a while. I won't be gone long."

Bob Overmile shook his head sadly and murmured: "Don't worry about me, friend. I'll stay right here and nurse this here beer. You go on and get your chops whacked. I don't want any of it."

Kerry grinned and went out, turning right at the next corner and navigating the length of a quiet residential street. Mary Owen kept a room at Mrs. Daniel's rooming house on the corner of Elm Street. Bert paused before the squeaky gate, then opened it, and went up the darkened path. The evening was warm and a gentle breeze whispered through the oaks shielding the lawn. Mrs. Daniel rocked on her porch, suddenly halting the motion of her chair. "Land's sake," she exclaimed, "Bert Kerry! I thought you'd gone for good." She was a heavy woman with iron-gray hair, and the years had given her an understanding that was rare.

Bert flopped down on the top step and twirled his hat in his hands. He nodded toward the interior of the house and said: "She home?"

"She's still mad at you," Mrs. Daniel said, ". . . or so she says, but I know better." She gave a snort of disgust and added: "That Milo . . . always hangin' around. Seems to me a girl that's twenty-three would have enough sense to see through a man like that."

"Mind if I go in?"

"Heavens, no," she said. "I been sittin' here night after night for a month hopin' you'd come back. I don't like a man that gives up easy."

"Give up?" Bert said. "What the hell's that?" He

got up and went into the house. The hall was flooded with lamplight, and he turned and mounted the stairs to her room on the upper floor. Light came from under her door, and he rapped softly.

Her footsteps came, clear and sharp, and she opened the door, gasped, then tried to close it quickly. Bert put out a beefy hand, holding it against her small strength and pleaded: "Mary, listen to me . . . please."

"Go away," she said, but her voice lacked conviction. "You're nothing but trouble."

"I only wanted to ask you to go to the dance with me," Bert said.

"I'm going with Milo Weeks, thank you," she said, but he noticed that she no longer tried to close the door. She sure was pretty, Bert thought. About as big as a pinch of salt, but she curved where a woman ought to curve. Her eyes were large and brown, and she had a whale of a temper.

"How about savin' me a couple of them dances then?" Bert asked. She considered this for a moment and shook her head. "Why not?" he wanted to know. "I can dance as good as that tanglefooted saddle bum."

She agreed with this. "You can fight, too," she supplied. "When Ray Dunlap called, you punched him in the nose. Harry Simmons left town after talking to you. There's something about you that worries me." She stood aside, and he came into her room. She left the door ajar, and he found that he had suddenly grown another left foot and didn't know where to put it.

"Bert," she said seriously, "it isn't that I don't like you, it's . . . well, you're so impulsive, and . . . and a little violent. Sometimes it frightens me . . . the way you do things. People talk, Bert. You're so blamed stubborn, and you've such a temper." She saw that she was making a very poor impression on him and switched her tactics. "I'm the schoolteacher . . . I have certain rules of conduct that I must adhere to. The last time I went for a buggy ride with you, we didn't get home until three in the morning. I don't know what I'd have done if Missus Daniel hadn't smoothed it over with the school board."

"You had fun, though, didn't you?"

She let out a long sigh and said: "Yes, Bert, I did, but can't you see . . . that isn't the point. We can't go through life just having fun."

"Why?" Bert asked. "Am I supposed to go around sad-faced and serious?"

"I told you how it is," she offered lamely.

"Shucks," he said, "things'll be different after we're married."

Color streamed into her face, and she turned away from him. Her voice was small and a little pleased. "I didn't know you had thoughts like that, Bert."

"Well, I have," he told her. "I . . . I love you, and

140

that's all there is to it. I ain't a man to give up easy."

It was a moment before she spoke, then her voice was torn with indecision. "You make me so confused sometimes. I . . . you're such a blunt man."

He thought about it and decided that she was like a skittish horse. He'd have to be careful and patient to bring her up on the rope. "I'll see you at the dance," he said, and turned and left the room. She came and stood in the doorway as he started down the stairs.

"Bert," she called softly, and he stopped quickly, his blunt face full of hope. "Please don't fight."

"Oh," he said, and went down the steps. Mrs. Daniel still sat in her rocker, and he paused on the edge of the porch. He listened to the sounds drifting from Custer Street and murmured: "Saturday night . . . there ain't any other night like it." He peeled a wrapper from a long cigar and got it ignited before adding: "Seems that a man'll work his fool head off all week long, but when Saturday night comes, he wants to beat his chest and howl at the moon."

"More to life than that," Mrs. Daniel said.

"Sure," Bert agreed, "but howlin' is more fun." He drew deeply on his smoke, content with the world, but then the gate *squeaked,* and his manner changed, and his face became stubborn and unbending.

Milo Weeks came to within three steps of the

porch before he recognized Bert Kerry. He brought himself up short, his smooth face covered with a displeased scowl. "Don't you ever get enough?" he asked in a slightly incredulous voice.

"Tell you how it is," Bert said. "When it gets too tough for the rest of the world, then it's just right for me." He grinned, and Milo's face filled with a sudden temper.

The man was tall and heavy-featured with hair, thick and wavy, and lips bold and curling below a slightly hooked nose. He fashioned a smoke with his legs spread apart, clearly a man with little give to his temper. He said shortly: "Don't make any mistakes tonight, Kerry. We'll be watching for 'em."

"I can blow my own nose," Kerry told him. "You just take care of yourself."

"Don't worry about it," Milo said. "This is my town. I'm on home ground here." He pushed rudely past Bert, jarring him with his shoulder, and went into the house.

Bert half turned to follow him with his eyes, and Mrs. Daniel swung his attention around when she said: "You just keep away from that man, Bert Kerry!"

"I never give a promise I can't keep," he told her, and walked down the darkened path, swinging immediately toward Custer Street and Garfinkle's Saloon.

Bob Overmile still sagged against the bar, his

half empty beer mug before him; Marshal Burk stood at his side in earnest conversation. Bert Kerry sided them and slapped the bar to draw Garfinkle's attention. Overmile studied him with a large question in his eyes and, when he saw no redness on Bert's cheeks, said: "Hail the conquering hero."

Bert took his beer and drank deeply, then said: "This is my night . . . I can feel it in my bones."

"Careful you don't get any broke," Frank Burk cautioned. "Milo can play rough when he has a few friends behind him."

Bert gave him a very pained look and said: "I am a man of peace. Live and let live is my motto."

Frank Burk sighed and murmured: "All right . . . bullhead. Don't say you haven't been warned." He turned away from the bar and passed through the crowd. Bert watched him until he went out of the door.

"What happened?" Overmile's voice was eager.

"Damned if I know," Bert confided. "Milo's still shovin' his handsome face into the picture, and at the moment I'm on the outside lookin' in. I can't help feelin' that that gal feels a hell of a lot more'n she lets on." He glanced at the wall clock, noticing that it was well after eight, and added: "Let's be on our way." He finished his beer in hurried gulps, and together they forced their way through the gathering crowd and out into the night.

II

The schoolhouse sat on a two-acre plot behind Race Street, and they left Custer, crossing a vacant lot before angling toward the lighted building. Buggies dotted the playground. Men made dark shapes along the edge of the building with the tips of their cigars glowing and dying; talk rose and fell in soft murmurs. Inside, bunting and decorations hung from the ceiling. The refreshment table stood along the east wall with the preacher and his wife standing guard over the punch bowl to prevent the introduction of hard liquor.

The room was crowded with people standing in friendly knots, talking and laughing. Bert and Overmile passed among them, getting friendly nods, occasionally a word of greeting. They drew stares and some open belligerence from the younger men, but Bert pretended not to notice it. The musicians arrived, a four-piece string orchestra, and spent a noisy five minutes arriving at a mutual key. There was a little foot tapping, then they swung into "Dixie" and the dance began. Kerry stayed near the stag line. Overmile leaned against the wall, his thin face slightly bored. Mary Owen arrived on Milo's arm and immediately they swung onto the floor.

Bert idled an hour away, listening to the music and the sound of capering feet. At last the mood caught him, and he pushed himself away from the wall and cut out onto the dance floor. The music ended, announcing the finish of a set, and Bert saw her across the room. Milo was smiling and perspiring, and Bert pushed past him to stand between them with his back to the big man. "Time for that dance?" he asked her.

Mary's pert face mirrored a moment's hesitation, then she looked past Kerry and saw Milo's face. "Yes," she said, almost eagerly, and took his arm, pulling him away.

Milo was not to be left out, and he took a quick step and caught Kerry on the arm. "Just a minute, friend," he said. "This is a peaceful gathering, and I for one wouldn't want trouble, but if you care to step outside sometime this evening, I'll give you a little of it."

The offer of a fight was an appealing thing to Bert, but the girl sensed it and pulled at him, and Bert said: "Later. Right now I'm gonna dance." The band struck up a lively tune, and he moved onto the floor. Milo Weeks was the furthest thing from his mind.

The worry never left her face, and she said: "Why do you think you have to lick the world? Accept every challenge that's hurled at you?"

Bert grinned and murmured: "Gosh, I ain't got to 'em all yet."

The corners of her mouth pulled down in disapproval, but he felt that she was secretly pleased with him. He whirled her and spotted an open side door, guiding her toward it. She made no protest when they stopped near it, and it gave him encouragement; they went out into the night coolness with nothing but the blackness and the sounds of laughter touching them.

She smoothed her dress and sat down on the steps. He stood above her and the strong call of her pulled at him, making him brash and slightly bold. He took her hand and, when she made no attempt to pull away, knelt before her and said: "Mary, why do we tell ourselves that it's wrong to love each other?"

She had her desires and her yearnings, but the strict propriety in her background executed considerable control over her, and she said half sharply: "You presume a great deal, Bert Kerry."

"Honey," Bert said, "all I can offer you is a ranch foreman's pay and a small house and a lot of hard work. Maybe that's wrong, but I ain't got better sense than to think a woman in love would find that enough." He searched her face in the darkness for some clue, but found none. He didn't find rejection, either, and it gave him hope. "Honey . . . do you love me?"

There was no lie in her, he knew that and perhaps was unfair with his question, but time was something he had little of. She said in a very small voice: "Yes . . . I love you, Bert."

"Then pack your things, and I'll rent a rig, and we'll leave tonight. Old man Carruthers is in there. He's the head of the school board. Tell him you're gonna quit, and that's all there is to it."

She clasped her hands together and closed her eyes, and he saw then that it was her desire, but that strictness came into her again and she was torn in her beliefs. "I can't, Bert . . . I can't. I want to, but it's impossible. Don't you see, it's the difference between us. You do things on impulse and maybe they turn out all right, but I'm afraid to live like that . . . I couldn't live like that. I'd have to know that there was something in you that responded to logic. I'm sorry that I'm the way I am, but I can't help it. Life isn't something to be hogged. It has to be lived slowly and sedately to be enjoyed."

It was the end of talk for him; he saw the uselessness of it and pulled her to her feet, wrapping his arms hungrily about her. She melted against him instinctively, before her propriety asserted itself. He kissed her long and fervently. Her fingers bit into the back of his neck, and she moaned softly as he released her

"Now," Bert said, "what was sedate about that? Love isn't mild like a glass of warm water before going to bed. It's fire and passion and hate and wickedness all rolled into a ball. Why do you hold back against something you really want?"

It took her a moment to regain her control, and her voice was unsteady when she used it. "We can't change ourselves, Bert. I'm sorry because I'm the way I am."

"That's a lame excuse," he said. "If you was any different from what you are, then I wouldn't give you a second look."

She placed her palms against his chest, and it was an embrace, so much emotion filled her voice. "Darling . . . you're like the wind, wild and free. You excite me . . . just being near you, but it takes more than just that. You're everything I want, yet not what I want. Sometimes you're so unbending . . . so self-willed, that I'm afraid." She turned from him and went up the short steps to pause in the lighted door. "Maybe we'd better not dance again this evening. I don't think it's wise."

He said nothing, and she went inside and was immediately lost in the crowd. He found another cigar in an inner pocket and lighted it, drawing deeply on the biting smoke. He stood thus for a few minutes, then became acutely conscious of not being alone. A shadow detached itself from along the side of the building, then three more stepped away.

Milo Weeks moved into the edge of the light and said tightly: "Tonight you stepped 'way out of line, Kerry."

The old temper and rashness returned in tumbling waves, and he said: "Why don't you put me back then."

"I intend to," Milo said, and turned to one of the men with him. "Get out front where you can see if anyone's comin'. I don't want to be disturbed once I get started."

The man trotted away, and Milo removed his coat and string tie, then made a great show of rolling his sleeves. The two men with him stood slightly to the rear and one side. Bert threw his cigar away and stepped down from the porch until he was even with Milo. Milo said: "No hard feelings, Kerry. Let's make this a friendly fight." He stuck out his hand.

Being the kind of a man he was, Bert reached for it, glancing down at it at the same time, and Milo stretched him flat with one punch. Instinct made Kerry roll, and Milo's kick went wild. Bert regained his feet in a swoop before the big man could reset himself. An anger burned now in Kerry's eyes and he dashed the blood away from his mouth and said: "Milo, from here on in it's gonna get rough."

If there was any fear in Kerry, it didn't show. He bore into the heavier man with a singleness of purpose that made Milo give ground. For a moment it was give and take, then Kerry hit the big man with a wicked punch, rocking him back on his heels. Milo tried to cover himself, but Kerry flattened him and stood back, waiting for him to get up.

Milo rolled over and gained his hands and knees, then lifted his head and looked at his two friends. Kerry sensed the signal and whirled, but they were on him and he went to the ground beneath their weight. He got in his licks, but they hoisted him to his feet between them, and Milo shuffled forward, his fists cocked. "I know how to handle a cocky buzzard. You want to play dirty . . . all right, then, we'll play dirty." He sledged Kerry along the shelf of the jaw.

He hit him again, this time in the pit of the stomach, turning as the look-out came charging across the schoolyard. "Let's go," he said breathlessly. "Frank Burk's comin' down the street, and, if he finds us fightin', we'll all land in the pokey." He looked at Kerry, still held between the two men and said with a great deal of heat: "What the hell, Milo . . . can't you whip him by yourself?"

The big man murmured something biting and turned away. The others freed Kerry and shoved him, face first, into some shrubbery. He watched them leave hurriedly and sat there, a large ache in his head and a wild stubbornness building up within him. He saw the marshal enter the schoolhouse, then rose, and went around to the back and washed his face in the well. His jaw was a solid ache, but he paid no attention to it, walking instead to the front door and reëntering.

He saw Milo and his friends by the west wall. Overmile saw Kerry come in and moved toward him, intercepting him. He whistled softly when he saw the bruise and said: "What the hell happened?"

Bert told him in a dozen tight phrases, and Overmile jerked his head around and gave Milo a long look. The big man's back was toward them, and Bert murmured: "Stick around and see that nobody jumps me from behind. I got business to attend to." He moved away, and Overmile followed three paces behind him.

Bert searched the room until he spotted the marshal against the other wall, then cut through the crowd, coming up to Milo from the side. There was a lull in the dancing. People gathered in clusters, talking and lifting their glasses of punch. Bert skirted them and touched Milo on the arm, bringing the big man around with a start.

"We didn't get to finish our dance, honey," Bert said, and knocked him against the wall. An open window came down with a loud *bang,* heads swiveled, and Frank Burk hurried through the crowd, using his shoulders and elbows. Milo stayed back against the wall, the blood bright on his lips, his hands flat against the boards. He made no move, and Kerry wheeled as Burk snapped: "Dammit, who the devil started this?"

Mary Owen was standing away from them

amid a group of shocked ladies. There was a heavy disapproval on her face when Bert glanced at her and she pulled her eyes away. Milo pointed to Kerry and said: "He did! I was standing here, minding my own business when he up and hits me."

Frank Burk looked at Kerry and there was no humor in the lawman's eyes. "Well?"

"He's lyin'," Bert proclaimed. "We tangled outside before you came, and he left it unfinished."

Burk was no fool, and he was an old hand at this sort of thing. He saw the bruise on Kerry's jaw and the swelling along the bottom lip. He drew his conclusions and said: "I told you what to do when you came to town. Do I hafta lock you up to keep the peace?"

Kerry ignored him and said: "This ain't the end of this, Milo."

The big man's face became holy, and he pleaded with the marshal. "You know that I want peace. Why do we have to put up with these wild ones from some other town who come here just to make trouble?"

Frank Burk's head came around quickly and he said with a great deal of bluntness: "This is a free country, Weeks. A man can come and go pretty much as he pleases as long as he behaves himself. I know you, and I don't think any more need be said."

Milo turned sulky.

Burk took Kerry by the arm. "Now, you leave here and don't give us any more trouble tonight."

"You call this justice?" Bert said heavily.

"I'm not arguing with you," Burk insisted. "I'm just telling you to behave yourself. Things have a way of evening themselves up."

"That's too slow for me," Kerry said, but he gave the marshal no more argument and left the schoolhouse. He paused on the outside and stood along the wall in the deep shadows. Overmile joined him and they stood in silence for a long time.

Finally Overmile said: "What's next?"

"What do you think?"

The skinny man shook his head and murmured: "Don't be a damn' fool. Burk's a square shooter, and you know it. Let that kinky-haired pretty boy alone. He'll get his."

"I want to give it to him," Bert insisted.

Overmile sighed and said: "That's just the trouble . . . you want to give it to him. Hell, take the lump and let someone else do it. Take it easy . . . a lot easier."

"I ain't made that way," Kerry stated.

"Then you better change, 'cause you're in for trouble before you die if you don't."

Kerry shot him an affronted stare and said: "You ain't old enough to be so damn' wise. If you wanna preach, go find yourself a cracker

153

barrel." He waited to see whether Overmile had anything further to say and, when he didn't, went around the building to the back door.

He looked both ways and, seeing no one, stepped onto the low porch. A red end of a cigar glowed and faded, and Frank Burk said—"Not tonight, Kerry."—and stepped out into the light. Kerry's blunt face was heavy with stubbornness and the marshal added: "Get off the prod, son. It ain't the way to win the war."

"You tell me a better way," Kerry demanded.

Burk sighed and said: "There ain't any way, boy. Some battles you gotta lose. You can't fight 'em all."

"I can try," Bert insisted.

There was no arguing with him, the marshal saw that, and motioned with his hand. "Go on . . . get uptown." He waited, and Bert swung away, going toward the front.

Overmile had gone back into the schoolhouse, and Bert went around the other side of the building and found a small wing with a window that was unlocked. He saw that no one was around and shoved it open and pulled himself in. He dangled for a moment, half in and half out, then disappeared inside. He found himself in the cloakroom and inched his way through the darkness until he found the door. He turned the knob slowly and peered through the crack into the lighted schoolroom. Refreshments were still being served; the table was not more than eight feet away from him.

He waited and watched the crowd mill around the room, then Frank Burk passed before the door, touching a man Kerry couldn't see. The marshal said: "I guess he's gone. I walked around the building, but I didn't see him. Overmile is still around, though. Let's have no trouble with him, understand?"

Bert pulled in his breath sharply as Milo Weeks said: "Thanks, Marshal. You don't have to worry about any of us."

Frank Burk was an independent man, and his voice turned brittle as he said: "You go straight to hell, Milo. I don't give a damn who kicks your face in, only I don't want a brawl here tonight." He placed his cigar firmly between his teeth and walked away.

Kerry waited a moment longer, half listening to the crowd, waiting to hear Milo speak again as an assurance that he hadn't moved away. He heard it, the low drawl, and shoved the door open and stepped onto the main floor. The big man turned in surprise, and Kerry was on him, lashing out with his fist.

He caught Milo flushly on the mouth, then one of Milo's friends made a vague pass, and Bert spun, knocking the man asprawl with a wild clout to the side of the head. Men shouted, a woman screamed, and a long cry went up. "Marshal! Fight!"

Milo came at Kerry as he half turned away, but the young man ducked low and loosened the man's teeth with an updriving punch. A man leaped astride Kerry from behind, bearing him to the floor, then another took hold of him, and they hoisted him to his feet, struggling wildly but securely held between them.

Milo saw Bert's momentary helplessness and stung him with an angry blow to the cheek bone. Frank Burk roughly forced his way through the crowd and blocked Milo's next effort. The big man forgot himself for a moment and gave the marshal considerable resistance, but Burk was an old hand and slapped the big man heavily and pushed him back until he was against the wall. "No more of that," he said, and Milo quieted.

Bob Overmile had observed this from his station along the wall across the room and came over. He looked at one of the men holding Kerry and said softly: "Let go of him."

The man gave him a short glance that said—*Mind your own damn business!*—and Bob took him by the collar and knocked him free with one punch. Frank Burk had turned in time to see this, and he gave Overmile a narrow glance. "You dealin' yourself in this?"

"I always been in," Bob said, and looked at the man on Bert's right. "Do I have to knock you loose, too?" he asked, and the man stepped back, glad to be out of it.

The marshal faced Kerry and said: "What does it take to make you quit?" Kerry gave him no answer, and Burk added: "I can throw you in the pokey until you cool off."

"Don't be a jackass, Bert," Overmile said. "Tell him what happened."

Kerry shook his head and told the marshal: "Go ahead and lock me up, but when I get out, I'll be after Milo again. He started something. Now let's see him finish it."

Someone in the crowd grew impatient and called out: "Hell, let 'em fight!"

The marshal reached a decision then and turned to Milo. "I know both of you roosters. Go on outside and finish it so we can have a dance here." Most of the men approved of this and said so with loud catcalls and an isolated Rebel yell. The jug had gone around several times behind the pickets, and blood clamored for a good fight.

Milo looked at the marshal for a long moment and said: "A hell of a thing for a lawman to say! You're supposed to keep the peace."

"I'm trying to," Frank Burk maintained. "We sure won't have any until you two settle this."

"I wouldn't dirty my hands on him," Milo said.

A howl of protest went up.

The marshal said quietly: "Looks like it's out of your hands now, Milo. Better go on outside."

The big man looked around at the people he knew, then said: "Like a bunch of dogs, waitin' for a fight." No one answered him, and an uneasy quiet settled over the room. Milo measured it in his mind and didn't like it, but there it was, and there was nothing he could do about it. He moved his heavy shoulders and said: "To hell with it. I can whip him just as easy right here."

It was what they wanted to hear, and they murmured among themselves, and formed a twenty foot circle around Kerry and the big man. The musicians left the bandstand, pushing and elbowing for a place in the front row. Milo looked at Kerry, and his temper flared, getting the best of him. "You saddle tramp . . . you got a lesson coming."

"Then give it to me," Bert said, and stepped into the big man. Milo's temper vanished, and he took a backward step. He forgot attack, trying only to defend himself against Kerry's whirlwind charge, and Kerry beat his defense aside and drove him to his knees. He backed away, and Milo took his time getting to his feet. Kerry moved in again, and, for a moment, Milo fought wildly, then went down under a sledging blow. He wasn't out, but he made no attempt to rise.

Bert stood back, motioning for the man to get up, but Milo shook his head. Kerry turned his head and looked at the marshal, and there was a frank disapproval in the lawman's eyes. Some of the men shuffled their feet uncomfortably; their home town boy was behaving badly and it galled.

Milo was not seriously hurt although the blood stood, red and bold, on his face. Bert Kerry said: "Get up and fight." Milo looked around him, half ashamed, but shook his head again. This produced a displeased muttering, and Kerry told him: "Say you've had enough."

"I've had enough," Milo said.

"Tell 'em you've been licked," Kerry ordered.

Men grew uncomfortable, and one in the back said—"A hell of a note."—and a low buzz filled the room.

Bob Overmile said: "Leave him alone, Bert."

"I ain't through," Bert said hotly.

"Yes, you are," Bob said, and his voice had suddenly grown slightly dangerous. Bert looked at him, then the fairness within him pushed at him, and he said: "You're right. I had no right to do that."

He turned suddenly and shoved his way through the ring of men. He headed for the nearest exit, the open side door across the room. He stepped out into the night, Overmile behind him. He had taken three steps when Mary Owen's voice halted him. "Just a minute, Bert!"

He stopped so quickly that Overmile rammed into him. The lean man glanced at the girl, then at Kerry, and moved away, pausing in the deep shadows along the building, out of earshot. Mary Owen's face was severe with anger and she took Bert firmly by the arms and tried to shake him. "Aren't you proud of yourself?" she said.

"No, I ain't," Bert admitted. There was a sincerity in his voice that took her back, but only for a moment.

She possessed a will, a stubbornness as strong as his own, and, once started, a thing was not put down until it was finished. "Do you want to know why I won't marry you? Well, I can tell you now. There is no unbending . . . no forgiveness in you. It wouldn't work because you never learned to take a slap in the face without giving one back."

"You know how it started," Bert said.

She made a disgusted motion and snapped: "Do you think I'm a fool? I know Milo . . . what kind of a man he is. I know of the threats he made against you around town, but I was glad he did. I wanted him to pick this fight, but I also hoped you'd rise above it and forget that it happened. I wanted to see if you had that in you, Bert." She made a small clucking noise with her lips and added: "What you did is bad. Milo is unpopular, but he is from Wineglass, and the townsmen will side him right or wrong. You struck at their pride when you made him quit. It was the wrong thing . . . believe me."

"I guess I had enough for one night," Bert said, and turned away from her.

III

Overmile left the shadows and joined him in silence. They walked to Custer Street and down its length and entered Garfinkle's Saloon.

A major portion of Wineglass' society was at the dance, and Garfinkle was enjoying a little lull in his business. They leaned against the bar, and Garfinkle drew two beers without comment and placed them before them. He saw the bruises on Kerry's face and murmured: "How does Milo look?"

Bob shook his head and said—*Lay off.*—with his eyes, and Garfinkle went to the other end of the bar.

They drank in silence for a few minutes, then Bert Kerry asked suddenly: "What's the matter with me, Bob?"

"You want an honest answer, or do you want me to make you feel good?" Bert shot him a distasteful glance, and Overmile went on: "Roughly, nothin' a good kick in the teeth wouldn't cure."

"Go ahead and kick me," Kerry invited.

Overmile shook his head. "Goes deeper than that. You go at things like a bull elk in ruttin' season. You do as you damned please . . . but that only works just so long, then you gotta do something that hurts like hell. Take Mary . . . you

161

saw her and liked her and tried to convince her in ten minutes that you should be the only man in her life. People don't grow like that . . . only Bert Kerry does."

Bert sipped his beer and retreated deeper into his thoughts. Bob Overmile opened his mouth to say more, then shrugged when he saw the look on Kerry's face, and waggled his finger for a refill. The saloon door opened and Frank Burk came in, giving the room a sweeping glance. He saw the two men standing alone and came alongside of them.

He glanced at Overmile, then at Kerry, and it was to him that he said: "Buck up . . . the night ain't over yet."

There was something in the man's voice that caused Kerry to break away from his thoughts, and he raised his head to give the marshal a searching glance. Frank Burk ordered a drink, saying nothing until Garfinkle placed it before him and went to the other end of the bar. "The boys got pretty rough with Milo after you left."

"Oh?"

"Yeah," Burke said. "Milo's friend . . . the one who was on look-out earlier in the evening . . . spilled it about how Jack and Ray held your arms while Milo slugged you in the teeth. Some of the younger bucks took him down to the pond and ducked him good." He glanced at Kerry and saw that his blunt face was severe.

"Hell," he added, "I thought you'd be glad to hear it."

Kerry leaned on the bar and idly twirled his glass. "All my life," he said, "I've fought my own fights, but this one I wish to hell I'd let slide by. Right now, I got a hold of somethin' I can't handle, and the harder I try, the deeper I get." He slapped the bar heavily and added: "Dammit, I want to marry that girl!"

Burk smiled and said: "Off the record, I'd like to see you do it, but you ain't gonna make her fall for you by kickin' hell outta her boyfriends." Bert opened his mouth to protest and the marshal said: "Shut up and let me finish! Now, let's look at this thing with a little sense for a change. Mary's a pretty thing, but she's an awful prude. Maybe she liked you right off, but she couldn't come up like some dame outta a dance hall and give you a big hug. However, if she collected a string of boyfriends . . . well, there's nothin' like competition to stimulate another man into thinkin' about weddin' bells."

"So you went and punched 'em in the nose," Overmile said.

"Hell," Bert snapped, "I didn't want them slobs hangin' around and beatin' my time! I know we'd make a go of it if she'd get over bein' so danged stubborn and say yes."

"Women," Frank Burk confided, "is funny sometimes. When a man says he understands women, then you know you're talkin' to a damned liar. A woman will go south when she wants to go north. She buys a hat she don't need to impress a man she wouldn't have on a bet. She'll bat her eyelashes at a stranger on a train and raise holy hell if he gives her a little squeeze." The marshal shook his head regretfully. "I seen 'em all . . . from A to Z . . . and I can tell you that it's been quite an education."

"She thinks I'm a roughneck," Bert maintained.

"She's right," Overmile said.

"You shut up," Bert told him. "I'm talkin' to this gentleman about a delicate subject."

"Sure she does," Burk agreed. "That's the kind of a man she wants, but take a little advice . . . don't have quite so much salt on. They like to mother a man a little. They want a brute when they're bein' chased, but when they put their rope on you, then they want somethin' nice and tame."

"I don't need a mother," Kerry said, "a wife's what I want."

The marshal let out an exasperated breath and rolled his eyes toward the ceiling. He finished his beer and stated: "Some men have to learn the hard way." He made a move as if to turn away and added: "Come over to the jail and get your gun. Milo said he was gonna kill you for what you done to him."

For the first time, Kerry showed a genuine

worry. "The crazy fool! I don't want no part in a shootin'! No part at all!"

The marshal tapped him on the chest with a forefinger and said: "You play rough, Bert. You gotta expect this sooner or later. Milo ain't much, but you pushed him even farther down. Now he wants to come back, and there's only one way for him to do it. You'd better pick up your gun."

Bert stood silent for a full minute, then said in a bare whisper: "All right. I'll be over."

"Don't waste too much time," Burk cautioned, and went out.

Bert finished his beer.

Overmile studied him at length and said: "We should have stayed in Hondo."

"For once," Kerry said with surprising seriousness, "you're dead right." He turned then, and Overmile turned with him, and they walked out into the night and across the street to the jail.

"I hate to see a thing like this," Burk said, and handed Kerry his gun. The young man spread the spring of his shoulder holster and nestled the weapon under his arm. Burk continued: "There's always men like Milo . . . full of fight talk, but somehow they lack the sand to cut it, or the good sense to leave well enough alone. Usually it ends up like this . . . with guns . . . and one of them is stretched out, and the other man is sorry."

Kerry listened to this, his face worried, then said: "You ain't makin' it any better by talkin' about it."

"Nobody said it was good," the marshal stated. "I've killed my man, and, even when he deserved it the worse way, I always wondered if I made a mistake somewhere and could have done it without shootin'."

Bert gave it some thought and murmured: "Something I never knew before . . . that a man could win and lose at the same time."

"For every victory, there's a price," the marshal said, and lighted a cigar. He looked at Bob Overmile and said: "You stay here until it's over."

The thin man's eyes widened. "What the devil?"

"He's got enough trouble," Burk said. "Milo's one of those crazy guys who stands in front of a mirror every day and practices his draw. I don't know's he's ever shot a man, but you never can tell about a man like that. You stay here just the same."

Kerry acted like he hadn't heard this. He said: "I'm going over to Missus Daniel's and see Mary."

"You'll be wastin' your time," Burk told him.

Kerry gave him a lopsided smile and said: "Know of a better way to waste it?"

The marshal shook his head, and Bert stepped

166

onto the darkened boardwalk, then walked down the street. When he turned the corner, he could see the schoolhouse. The dance had broken up early; men were drifting uptown, seeking strategic positions along Custer Street.

A small lamp glowed in Mrs. Daniel's hall, shedding a faint light over the vine-covered porch. He opened the gate, and low voices stopped. Nothing was said until he touched the bottom step, then Mrs. Daniel's surprised voice: "Land's sake, Bert Kerry. Haven't you any better sense than to be on the street?" She glanced at Mary, then rose and added—"It's past my bedtime."—and went into the house.

A silence fell between them and Bert said softly: "I didn't want this . . . I want you to know that."

She rose and came off the porch to touch him and her voice was husky. "Bert . . . if you love me . . . get on your horse and ride out."

He was shocked that she could ask such a thing. He said: "Run? From that fancy-pants bluffer?"

"Would you rather kill him, than sacrifice that much of your pride?"

He found himself confronted with a woman's logic, and he didn't know what to do about it. He studied her face in the meager light and said: "Tell me what to do, Mary. I honestly don't know."

The decision was hard for her, but she had a will and drew upon it. "I won't tell you, Bert. It's something you must decide for yourself. I can make it easy for you, but I have a future at stake. If I must gamble . . . I'd rather gamble now." She clasped her hands together in a half-fearful gesture and added: "I have to know what kind of a man you really are, Bert . . . I just have to know." She saw the look on his face, and it shattered her reserve. "Bert . . . Bert, don't hate me . . . please, don't hate me."

He gathered her into his arms because words were not in him, but she was a wise woman and understood the fervency of his embrace. He released her at last and kissed her. There was nothing more to say; he understood that and left her, walking down the darkened path to town.

There was little fear in Bert Kerry, just a genuine puzzlement. He understood Milo better than the man understood himself because they were alike, only Kerry was more so. Knowing he was stronger than Milo left him with a strange feeling. He knew then how it would end; he felt it that strongly. He stopped suddenly as the thought struck him. If he was so sure, then Mary was equally sure because she possessed this knowledge of him. Overmile knew—and the marshal knew. Perhaps even the townsmen knew because they were at the schoolhouse when Milo knew shame. It gave him a jolt, forcing his mind to a decision, and he paused at a break between the buildings and drew his .38-40 from his shoulder holster and tossed it among the rubbish.

The decision gave him no relief, but he shrugged it off because habit was strong within him. He turned on Custer Street and walked to Garfinkle's Saloon. The town was unusually quiet although store windows were bright with lamplight. He mounted Garfinkle's short porch and went in. There were two dozen men in the room, and they all looked at him in unison, then shifted their eyes as he came against the bar. He ordered a beer, then glanced at the mirror behind the bar as Frank Burk entered. The marshal stopped by Bert's elbow and said softly: "He's down at Harry Wickbloom's Pool Hall. He's talkin' big, so maybe it'll blow over."

"You believe that?"

Burk shook his head. "Naw, I'm just talkin'. He's made too many brags to back down now."

Kerry turned his head and looked at the marshal for a long moment, then murmured: "You could stop this, you know."

"Maybe," Frank said, "but I don't want to." He studied his folded hands and added: "You're between the devil and the sweat. You can shoot him, then spend the rest of your life regretting it."

Bert's temper crowded into his face, and he said savagely: "What am I supposed to do . . . be a sitting duck?"

The marshal's face settled into tired lines and he said: "Do what's right, that's all."

"What's right?"

"I couldn't say. It differs with men."

Kerry lowered his head and thought: *What's he trying to tell me?* But he could find no answer. The marshal left him and joined a group clustered around a table along the west wall. Kerry finished his beer and ordered another, but he had no thirst.

Garfinkle eyed him with considerable concern and Kerry asked: "You, too?"

The saloonkeeper shrugged and murmured: "You're a good fella. A little wild, maybe." He polished an imaginary spot on the bar, wanting to say more, but held back by some force Kerry didn't understand. He looked around the room. They were all watching him, measuring him, it seemed, and he wondered why.

Garfinkle moved away, and then he was alone at the bar. Low voices filled the room, but he paid little attention. He swung around, undecided, then went out and crossed the street to the jail. The front door was open. Bob Overmile sat in the marshal's chair, looking at a stack of Reward dodgers.

He gave Bert a long look, then went back to his reading. Kerry sat on the edge of the desk and reached out a big hand, taking the dodgers away from Overmile, and tossed them on the floor.

"You ought not bother a man when he's readin'," Overmile said.

"I want a few answers," Bert stated.

"The only answers worth a hoot," Overmile said, "are the ones a man figures out for himself."

"I thought you was my friend?"

"The best you got," Bob told him.

Bert blew out a long breath and said: "What would you do if a man was prowlin' the streets for you?"

"Shoot him on sight," Bob said without hesitation, "because I'd be scared."

"I don't understand that," Bert admitted.

Overmile shrugged. "Something you gotta dig out for yourself." He bent down and retrieved the Reward dodgers and sorted through them until he found his place.

"Mary wanted me to ride out of town," Bert said.

"That's one way of doing it," Overmile opined.

"A hell of a thing for you to say!"

Overmile said: "It ain't me he's after."

"You're no help at all."

"Nobody is at a time like this," Overmile said, and looked at Kerry. The thing he had been feeling came up again and brushed him, but eluded him before he could contact it. Overmile tossed the dodgers on the desk and said: "A man ought to look through those. Some pretty young kids there with some bad records. Makes a man wonder what can happen to change a man into something like that. Makes him stop and wonder just how far bullheadedness can lead him."

"What're you tryin' to say?"

"Nothin' at all," Bob stated, and closed his friend out by leaning back in the marshal's chair and pulling his hat down over his eyes. Kerry stared at him a long moment, then crossed to the door and let himself out.

He stood on the edge of the boardwalk and gave the darkened street a glance. A half block down, light streamed from the open doors of Wickbloom's Pool Hall, then it darkened as a big man stepped out with a dozen men trailing him. Kerry pulled in his breath and held it. He stood rooted until Milo swung his head and saw him.

There was some hesitation in the big man, but his talk had pushed at him, and he stepped into the street, walking toward Kerry with slow strides. The men who followed Milo broke then and scattered along the boardwalk, well out of the line of fire. Milo's face was white and set, and he kept his thumb hooked in his gun belt. He halted ten feet from Kerry and said: "Tonight you made a lot of mistakes."

"It's all in the point of view," Kerry said in a voice that was strangely calm. He knew what he was going to do then and did it. He turned until he was quartered away from Milo, presenting his back to the man, and walked across the street.

Milo's heavy voice split the night. "Turn around. Kerry!"

Bert kept on walking. The thing that eluded him came sharper then, and he gained a faint wisdom. With it came fear, sharp and probing, and he tried to beat it down. He took another three steps, and Milo shouted: "For the last time . . . turn around!"

Kerry took the bottom step, then the next, then there was a shout, and a gun went off, and a heavy fist sledged into the small of his back, driving him forward onto the porch.

Men shouted in the street, and the marshal boiled out of Garfinkle's, almost stepping on Kerry. He heard Overmile's voice, and Milo's shouting: "You all saw him do it! He was reaching for it under his coat!"

Kerry felt himself being rolled over; it was Frank Burk that held him up. "Just take it easy," the marshal said, and the men crowded around him with Milo pushing his way to the front, the gun still dangling in his hand and a wild, glad look on his heavy face. He'd just shot a man and it wasn't so bad, not nearly as bad as he'd imagined, that much was plain on his face. Frank Burk reached under Kerry's coat, and his fingers touched the empty holster. He threw the coat back and all of the men saw it, too.

Milo's face fell and he looked around him uneasily. He said in a loud, bawling voice: "You men saw him pull! By God, it's around here! He had to drop it!"

Several men searched for the gun and, when they failed to find it, crowded against Milo, suddenly caught up in an ugly mood. Kerry kept his eyes focused on Frank Burk's face. He found it easier to ride the pain that way. One man bolted off the porch for the doctor. Overmile was by Kerry then and he said: "Where's your gun?"

Kerry made a weak motion. "I chucked it . . . an hour ago . . . between some buildings on Elm Street."

"He's lyin'!" Milo yelled. "He pulled first! You fellas seen him!"

One blunt-faced man growled: "I saw it all and Kerry's hands never left his sides. He was just walkin'."

Frank Burk nodded to two men, and they lifted Kerry and took him into Garfinkle's, laying him face down on a crap table. The crowd followed, shoving Milo ahead of them. Overmile turned and went out the door, heading for Mrs. Daniel's boarding house on Elm Street.

Milo said: "By God, don't nobody try to pin a killin' on me!"

The marshal whirled on him and struck him solidly in the mouth. He hit the big man again in the stomach, at the same time wrenching the gun from his hand and slashing him across the jaw with the butt. Milo would have fallen, but the men held him erect, and the marshal rocked him with another driving punch. Someone said— "That's enough, Frank."—and the lawman turned away, shaking.

The doctor forced his way through the crowd that packed the door, and a swamper came over with three lamps. The room suddenly smelled strongly of chloroform. The men backed away to give the doctor room. Milo's face was streaming blood, but the two men held him firmly.

The marshal faced him again and said with soft wickedness: "If that boy dies, I'm gonna slap the horse out from under you, so help me God."

"I thought he had a gun," Milo said weakly. "You'd think when a man was after him, he'd have sense enough to hang onto his gun."

"Shut your yella mouth!" Burk spat at him. "I've seen hundreds just like you . . . full of big talk and whiskey guts. You think you're tough, but you just shot a man who's tougher than you'll ever be. He never needed a gun to tame you." Burk lowered his voice and some of the wildness faded from his eyes. He told the men that held Milo: "Take him over to the jail and lock him up."

He turned on the crowd then, breaking them up with rough words, then turned back to the crap table and the doctor who sweat in the lamplight. Kerry still lay face down, slightly sick from the chloroform. A pan of bloody water sat on the floor; bloodstained towels lay in a sodden heap. Burk watched the doctor finish his bandaging and said: "How bad is he?"

"Young and tough . . . he'll live if he gets good care."

"He'll get it," Burk said, and it was a promise.

The doctor snapped the clasps on his bag and turned as the front doors parted. Bob Overmile entered, and Mary Owen was with him. She saw Bert and ran to him, and she was crying and holding his hand. Frank Burk said: "A saloon is no place for a schoolteacher, Mary."

"My place is where he is," she said, and brushed the hair from Kerry's damp forehead.

The effects of the chloroform were wearing off, and Bert opened his eyes, then closed them until the room stopped rotating. He tried again and found that they worked and looked at her. He managed a smile, and a weak voice. "I guess I don't want to lick the world, honey . . . too tough."

She pressed her lips against his cheek and murmured: "It's all right . . . everything's all right now."

Bert turned his head until the marshal came into the tail end of his vision and asked: "Did I do right?"

"You're the rightest thing I know," Burk said, and motioned to Overmile. They went out,

Overmile cutting toward the livery for a buckboard, the marshal standing on the saloon porch.

Bert gave his wandering attention to Mary and said: "I guess it takes a long time for anything to soak into me. I guess I was just a little ways from bein' a shootin' man and didn't know it." He smiled weakly and added: "I'm sure glad I ain't." The talk wore him out, but he knew that she understood, and that was all that mattered to him.

Two men came in with a litter, and they picked him up with a great gentleness and carried him outside to the waiting buckboard. Mary climbed in the back with him, and then he knew where he was going. From then on, he would always know where he was going.

The buckboard lurched once, then settled down to a steady motion. He closed his eyes against the pain and felt her hands and the buckboard's jolt, but he didn't mind it. He was a happy man.

LET'S ALL GO KILL THE SCARED OLD MAN

There is something about a telephone call at five o'clock in the morning that has always given me an eerie feeling. When it jangled, I sat bolt upright in bed, pawing the sleep from my eyes. There was no need to turn on the light. The summer sun was on its way.

I lifted the receiver. "Carney speaking."

"Les," a metallic voice said, "this is Harry Johnson at the sheriff's office. Can you come over right away?"

I looked at the clock. "At a quarter after five? What's up?" A mental picture of Harry flashed in my mind, a big man, forty, with a lazy man's bulge around his middle.

"There's been a little trouble," Harry said. "I don't want to talk over the phone. Just come over."

"All right," I told him, and cradled the receiver. I didn't bother to shower or shave, just slipped into a pair of suntans and sport shirt. Leaving the house a few minutes later, I walked along the quiet back street, then cut across the schoolyard to the courthouse. I had expected to see a broad alteration in New Hope's scheme of things when I came back from the war, but the town was unchanged. Untouched was a better word. I had slipped into my old job at the newspaper as if nothing had happened—no rationing, no shortages, no war. I don't suppose New Hope has changed in the last sixty years. Merchants pass their businesses on to their sons. Farms change hands the same way. Since New Hope is the county seat, we have a jail, but, except for an occasional chicken thief, the citizens manage to stay out of it.

You ask how a man can be happy putting out a weekly paper in a dead burg like this? After three years of island hopping and dodging bullets, New Hope, with its sleepy, retired atmosphere, looks good to me.

Going around to the side door, I entered the outer office that led into the jail. Deputy Harry Johnson was there with three other men I had known all my life. Each man had a rifle and was cramming shells into the magazines.

"Going hunting?" I asked, trying to make a joke out of something that instinct told me was no joking matter.

"That's it exactly," Harry Johnson said. He was sweating although the office was cool, the moisture running along the seams of his face. You've met men like Harry, the kind you dislike on sight, then wonder why. At one time I had blamed it on the badge and the authority it gave him, then later decided the reason lay obscured by many small things that were hard to pin down.

Harry gave me a sharp glance and said: "I want you along on this, Les. Get some first-hand dope for your paper."

"Along on what?" I turned my head to watch the three grim-faced men with the rifles.

Mopping his face with his sleeve, Harry said: "Sheriff Carver was shot not over an hour ago. Jonas Alves did it."

"Jonas? Why that old man wouldn't . . ."

"Well, he did!" Harry interrupted. "We're going out after him." He crossed to a wall rack and handed me an M1 rifle, along with a bandoleer of shells. "This will make it old home week for you," he added, and nodded toward the door.

The three men hefted their weapons awkwardly and filed outside. The county Plymouth was parked under an elm tree and I got in the front with Harry. The three men sat cramped together in the back, the muzzles of their guns pointing up.

Harry eased the car out of the yard and leaned on the siren when he turned onto the highway. We screamed through town, then took a dirt road that wound over the countryside. Iowa is a pretty place, full of white farmhouses and big red barns. Whitewashed fences break the land up into squares, alternating patches of black earth and green corn.

The land is rolling and the back roads were dusty after two weeks without rain. Harry drove with a reckless abandon. He liked to do everything this way, with a lot of muscle and not much care.

I knew the Jonas Alves place; I had spent my boyhood playing in the bend of the creek near his house. Harry rode the brakes hard and turned off on a narrow winding road that followed the roll of the hills and ended near the breast of a small hill. We got out of the car and stood around uncertainly. We, I said—not Harry Johnson.

"Now approach carefully," he said. "The old man's armed and dangerous." He made a fanning motion with his hand and the men scattered, but not too far.

A good infantry sergeant would have been booting rumps about then, driving them farther apart. Green troops in combat have the pack instinct because they are afraid, but soon learn it's safer to thin out. Harry motioned for me to follow him and lowered himself belly flat to peer over the crown of the hill.

Jonas Alves's place is in a hollow, a salt-box two-story house that paint hasn't touched for twenty years. A sagging barn sits behind it, plus an outhouse and tack shed. The remains of a pole fence circles the place, the wire long rusted away.

It was fifty yards to the porch, I judged, then noticed Alves's dog by the steps. The dog was dead and flies were beginning to gather.

Behind us, the sun started to climb and laid a

hot hand on our backs. Harry was sweating heavily and he licked his lips as he looked the place over.

I looked at the dog. I was remembering back ten years when Alves got the dog. A carnival hand was going to drown the pup and Alves talked him out of it. A ball of fur with shoe-button eyes and a pink tongue that kept licking the old man's face. That was the old man's big weakness, his reluctance to hurt anything. I suppose in his childish way, *his* world was full of good things, for he completely closed his mind to any other.

Harry Johnson touched me on the arm. "He's still in there. I saw him move past a window. How do you get a man out of a place like that, Les?"

"Go in and get him," I said. "Who killed the dog?" I rolled up my shirt sleeves. It was ninety and getting hotter.

"Carver," Harry Johnson said. He cupped his hands around his mouth. "Alves? You hear me? Come on out of there with your hands up!"

"What for?" I asked.

"What for what?" Harry's head came around quickly, irked by this interruption.

"Why did Carver kill the dog?"

"We got a complaint," he said. "The dog had been chasin' chickens. Carver came out to talk to Alves and Alves shot him with a Twenty-Two." He mopped at his face with his sleeve.

"Is that when the sheriff shot the dog?"

"Who cares about the dog?" He blew out his breath through his teeth. "Carver shot the dog first." He gave me a look that told me to drop the subject. "There's a killer down there and it's up to me to get him out. Alves!" he yelled. "You hear me, Alves? Come on out of there before we have to come in and get you!"

There was no sound from the old house. Nothing stirred except a few chickens moving around the yard, their heads bobbing as they scratched for feed. Behind the barn, two pigs quarreled over possession of a small mud puddle.

Shifting his bulk, Harry Johnson brought his pump shotgun around. He aimed, touched it off, and a window disappeared from the front of the house. Echoes sounded over the countryside and the chickens scattered, squawking loudly.

I grabbed him by the shoulder and pulled him around. "What the hell did you do that for? He'll be scared to come out now."

"He had his chance," Harry said, but in his eyes there was uncertainty, as though he wondered if he had made a mistake. But there was a badge on his shirt that covered this act and he took refuge behind it. "I'm the law here, Carney. If you don't like it, then go back to town."

"There was no need to shoot," I said.

"What do you want me to do?" he flared. "Sit up here in the sun and build a nest?" He licked his lips and stared at the house.

Charlie Carruthers, the man on my left, had been a special deputy for twenty years. I slid over to where he lay. He glanced at me and said: "Harry on the peck?"

"Something's pushing him," I said. "Getting hot out, isn't it?"

"It'll get hotter," Carruthers said. He was a rail-thin man with a farmer's face, darkly tanned and weather-lined. He fingered his rifle and peered over the lip of the hill. Nothing stirred below.

"What do you think happened?" I asked. "Between Carver and Jonas, I mean?"

"I couldn't say," Carruthers murmured. "Harry called me on the phone." He gave me a quick look, then his eyes slid away.

"The sheriff liked his little joke with the old man," I said. "This one could have got out of hand. Alves never *wanted* to harm anything."

"That's possible," Carruthers admitted, and stared at the house.

Harry Johnson looked our way and said: "Pour a few rounds in there. We'll smoke the old coot out."

Carruthers looked uncertain. He glanced at me, then at the other two special deputies on the other side of him. Carruthers's finger curled and uncurled around the trigger.

"Dammit!" Harry snapped. "Shoot!"

The man on the far end fired. The bullet slivered wood from Jonas Alves's front porch and then a ragged volley began, hitting nothing except the yard and front porch. Harry emptied his shotgun at the windows and, when there were no more squares of glass intact, pulled back and lay still, the sweat pouring off his face.

I glanced at him and thought: *You're warming up. You've got to build it all up inside before you can shoot a man.*

The sun was stronger now, a driving weight against our backs. The pigs were still quarreling over the mud puddle in back of the barn.

Carruthers was watching Harry Johnson now. He said: "What's got into him, Les? We'll never get him out this way." He licked his lips. "I don't like this, Les. Don't like it at all."

On the New Hope road, cars turned off onto Jonas Alves's lane. I looked around as the first one drove up and parked along the crest of a nearby hill. A man, his wife, and three children got out. The woman grabbed the children to keep them from running downhill toward us. A moment later two more cars drove up and stopped. Everyone got out and hunkered down for a clear view of the farmhouse.

Harry Johnson looked at this gathering, then turned again to Jonas Alves's house and yelled: "Old man! Come out of there, old man!"

"Maybe we got him," Charlie Carruthers said in a soft, awed voice.

"He's still alive," Harry snapped. "Pour some

lead in there. If you run out of shells, we got plenty more."

He crouched over his pump gun, refreshing the magazine while I lay back and looked around. Carruthers raised his rifle and pumped two fast shots into the house. The other two, Clarence Howland and Mel Griffin, added to this barrage.

With every shot it gets easier, I thought. Stay loose, they used to tell us in the Army. It wasn't until after my first fire fight that I really understood what the sergeant had meant. Carruthers and the others were finding out now. The first volley had been the hardest, but now they leaned back against the rise of earth, half pleased with themselves as they reloaded.

A siren wailed out on the main road, drawing nearer. Harry looked around quickly, and said: "Gold!" He was tense, like a dog whose food is threatened.

The state police car wheeled into the lane and parked beside the county Plymouth. Sergeant Harley Gold got out with two troopers. He came directly to Harry Johnson and said: "You could have at least called me. I got it over the AP teletype twenty minutes ago."

"We can handle it ourselves," Harry said, reloading his shotgun. "No sense in callin' you fellas. Better get down under cover. He's still there and he's got a gun."

Sergeant Gold deployed his men to disciplined

186

intervals. I could see the training behind this simple maneuver. The hypothetical field problems, the classroom lectures, all preparing them for this one moment. The meeting of man with his enemy.

One of the troopers had a Thompson sub-machine gun and he raised the blunt muzzle past the rise of earth, rattling a quick burst into the house.

Harry Johnson flipped his head around, shouting: "Knock that off!" He rolled over and faced Sergeant Gold. "*I'm* running this and don't you forget it!"

"All right," Gold said, " that's the way you want it." He lay belly flat in the dust, his .38 special in his hand. He glanced once at me and the unfired M1, then slitted his eyes against the bouncing heat and stared at the farmhouse.

Harry fired his shotgun twice, almost in blind rage, then yelled: "Jonas Alves! We know you're in there! Don't make me come in and get you!" He lay back then, sweating. "That damned sun's hot. We could use some water."

"There's a canteen in the car," Sergeant Gold said, and Harry went after it. Gold looked at me and said: "What are you doing here, Les?"

"You tell me."

Gold glanced over his shoulder at Harry who stood by the patrol car, the canteen tipped up. "What's got into *him?*"

"I'll let you know when I figure it out," I said.

Harry came back and took his position again. Gold said: "Are you sure he's in there?"

"He's in there," Harry said flatly.

I turned my head and looked at the growing crowd on the hillside. At least 100 people were gathered there now, holding newspapers over their heads as a shield against the blasting sun. I saw the butcher, still in his cuffs and white apron. The straw hats identified the farmers. Children ran along the rim, scuffing dust and calling to each other while the women huddled in one group, pointing and chattering.

"You ought to get those people out of there," Gold said.

"What for?" Harry said. "They're taxpayers. They got rights."

He signaled for another fusillade and emptied his shotgun at the front door, then lay back and fumbled for more shells. Sergeant Gold looked around. "What are you trying to do, Harry? Turn this into a shooting gallery?"

"I know what I'm doing," Harry said. Sweat ran into his eyes and he dashed it away, squinting against the glaring heat. I watched him closely now, for he was going through a change and I didn't fully understand it. In a way this was familiar to me, as though I had seen it before somewhere and couldn't remember where.

Sergeant Gold spoke to me. "You out of ammo?" He pointed to my rifle.

"I'll shoot when I see something," I told him, and he shrugged.

Noon came and went and the sun was a furnace. Mel Griffin went to a nearby farmhouse and brought back a milk can full of water, but thirty minutes in the sun made it too hot to drink.

The shooting continued until the front of the house was puckered with bullets and looked as though some outsize woodpecker had been working on it.

Sergeant Gold's forest green uniform was almost sweated through. All of us were hot and dusty, but no one paid any attention to this. They all stared at the farmhouse.

I watched Harry Johnson whose face was grimly set. The others watched him, puzzled, confused, but suddenly I wasn't confused any longer. I don't think Harry was seeing the farmhouse any more. He had that vacant, far-away expression in his eyes.

Sergeant Gold said: "Harry, this has gone far enough. Either you go in there and get him, or I will."

Johnson nodded, then turned to me. "What do you think, Les? You've softened up enough pillboxes. Is he ready yet?"

Up to this point I had wondered why I was here and now I knew. I was a veteran, the man who had walked through the fire, and Harry needed me. *Say what he wants to hear,* I thought. *That's the easy way.*

I stared at the hollow and Alves's battered house. There was no movement down there, nothing to indicate that he was alive. With all the shooting that had been going on, it was possible that he had been hit and had been dead for hours.

The same thing must have occurred to Harry Johnson, for he said: "Never mind. I'll go in and get him myself."

"I'll go with you," I told him, and laid aside the rifle and bandoleer of cartridges.

"I can do it alone," he said. He stared at me, telling me with his eyes to stay out of it.

But I couldn't do that, not knowing what I now knew. "It's no trouble," I assured him, and got up when he did. He didn't like it; I could tell by his dark glance. But I followed him anyway as he ran around the hill to where it tapered into a gully split by the creek. He was sweating heavily, and, when he stopped, his breath whistled through his nose.

"You don't have to come," he said again. "You're not a deputy." He saw then that I no longer had my rifle. "Where's your gun?"

"Too hot to lug around," I told him.

"I don't want you in there without a gun," he said.

Jonas Alves's house was thirty yards away, a clean run with the outhouse and tack shed to screen us in case he was watching from the side window. Harry looked it over carefully, wiping his sweating hands on his pant leg. He checked the shotgun three times, and I stood there, watching him trying to decide whether he could get away with it with me along.

Killing a man is never easy, not even when you're telling yourself all the things Harry must have been telling himself. This was legal. The man was armed and a fugitive. He could pass behind this curtain now and return to society untainted. How do I know? Because I did the same thing in the war. He was tasting the wine and liking it.

"I'll get him," he said again, and suddenly broke into a run.

He charged across the dusty yard, his hand-cuffs and keys jangling. I followed at his heels, and then we were on the sagging porch and he hit the door with 200 pounds of beef, carrying it off the hinges and crashing into the room.

Once inside, he halted, the snout of his shotgun swinging back and forth. The room held strong odors of dust and decay. Bullets had pierced the walls in a dozen places, bringing down sheets of plaster and torn shreds of flowered wallpaper.

A door stood open on our left and he stepped toward it, his shotgun cocked and ready. I moved right behind him, but I never looked into the room. I was watching Harry Johnson.

I saw the old man as Harry snapped the shot-gun to his shoulder. Jonas Alves was in the corner, kneeling, his face to the wall and his head pillowed in the ell where the walls joined. His thin shoulders were shaking and in the sudden silence his crying was clearly audible.

Across his knees lay his rifle, a rusted, single-shot Stevens .22. I don't think he knew that anyone else was in the room with him.

Harry yelled in a voice loud enough for the people on the hill to hear. "Throw up your hands!"

This will make it legal, I thought. *This has to be legal. No man could live with himself if it wasn't.*

Jonas Alves didn't move and I spoke softly. "He can't hear you, Harry. He's too scared."

Harry Johnson didn't hear me, either. Here was his quarry, cornered, but unwilling to give him the fight he needed, and by that unwillingness Jonas Alves was depriving him of his finest hour.

In the most meek man there is that subconscious urge to kill, and I recognized it in Harry's eyes, a glazed look that I could not mistake.

Lashing out with my arm, I drove the shotgun toward the ceiling as Harry Johnson pulled the trigger. Plaster came down in a shower and a gaping hole appeared.

He swung toward me, a confused, misguided rage in his eyes, and I hit him then in the mouth and sent him cascading into the wall. He lost his shotgun, and I kicked it under the bed.

"Now get out of here," I said, not raising my voice.

The shock of the blow calmed him and he wiped blood off his mouth. He stared at me, puzzled. "What the hell's got into you?"

I shook my head. *He really doesn't know*, I thought. The side of his personality that for a moment had been revealed was sealed off again, a blind spot he could neither see nor comprehend.

"Get out, Harry."

"I said what the hell's the matter with you, Les?" A slow flush crept up from his neck and suffused his cheeks. He blinked once or twice. "Didn't you hear what I asked you?"

I looked at him squarely, feeling a lump come up in my gorge and swallowing it down so that I could speak. I felt terrible.

"Get the god damn hell out of here, Harry," I said, as evenly as I could. "Just turn tail and go home."

He didn't argue, just turned to the door, confused. He stopped and turned for another puzzled look at me. *He thinks I've blown my top*, I thought, and almost smiled. *He'll always think that*. And that was the pitiable part, the fact that he would never understand what had happened to himself.

I bent and touched Jonas Alves on the arm and, when he stood up, led him outside into the drenching sunlight.

THE FIGHT AT RENEGADE BASIN

I

The cold dawn light was beginning to break the soot shadows of night when Ben Dembrow turned off the main trail, following a rough wagon road even higher into the rocks. Finally the road leveled and he splashed across a swift-moving creek. Ahead lay a cabin, the windows bright frosted squares of light. As he wheeled into the yard to dismount by the porch, the door opened and a man stood framed by the light.

"Come on in, Ben," he said, stepping aside. He was a small man, whiskered and aged by hard work and not enough money.

The cabin was warm and Ben shed his hat and coat, moving immediately to the cook stove. A young girl fried eggs and side meat. She gave Ben a glance when he edged near the heat. "Smile, Ben. They say it always helps."

Ben Dembrow looked at Elizabeth Wyatt for a moment, then said: "A man never smiles at his own funeral." He turned to the cupboard for a

194

cup, then poured some coffee for himself. Dave Wyatt was sitting on the edge of his chair, his legs outthrust, his attention never leaving Ben Dembrow.

"You decided to go through with it, Ben?"

"Got no choice now," Ben said. "I got eighty head of horses there, Dave. Too late in the year to move 'em, and danged if I want to, either. I proved up on that place and it's mine, legal as can be."

Elizabeth turned her head and looked at Ben Dembrow. She was a year or two younger than he, pretty and curvy, and very wise to the ways of men in trouble, for her father had known it all his homesteading life. "You made a deal with Anse Sonnerman, Ben."

"I made no deal," he said quickly. "None of us did." He paused for a moment. "I promised nothing to Anse Sonnerman. I followed orders, like the rest of them."

The eggs and side meat were done and Elizabeth filled a platter. Ben sat down at the table and Elizabeth took her place beside him. There was little talk until the coffee was poured. Then Dave Wyatt said: "Ben, we're your friends. You know that. But this is a time for plain talk."

Ben looked steadily at him. "Then talk plain, Dave."

Wyatt glanced at his daughter, then at Ben Dembrow. "In an hour and a half you've got to face Anse with your decision. Whether you can or can't is your business, but, Ben, we don't want trouble with Anse. Had enough trouble in my life. A little peace has spoiled me now."

"Keep talking," Ben invited. "You haven't made your point yet."

Dave Wyatt leaned back in his chair. "Ben, eight families are living up here beyond the pass where you are located. Eight families that don't want to take sides in any fight you have with Sonnerman."

"You're not in this," Ben said. "The whole thing is between Sonnerman and me."

Dave Wyatt shook his head. "You think it is, but it ain't. Tomorrow, after Sonnerman re-records the deeds he'll buy up today, that whole valley will be his. That's a lot of land, Ben. And a lot of power to the man that owns it." He waved his hand to include all the land. "This country is wild, Ben. Good for nothin' except in the small valleys such as this. But Sonnerman needs it for winter shelter. Needs it and uses it every year when he drives his herd through the pass." He leaned forward and spoke softly. "You're sittin' in the middle of that pass, Ben, and the question is, are you goin' to let Sonnerman through or not?"

"That's somethin' I ain't decided," Ben said.

"Better decide," Dave Wyatt said. "We'll want to know as bad as he does."

"I don't see where you come in, Dave." Then he

196

stopped and looked more sharply at the older man. "Sure, I see now. Sonnerman used to graze his cattle in these valleys. There was always good grass under the snow. But now those valleys are already homesteaded and he buys his hay from you." He got up slowly. "Looks like I've hit you folks where it hurts . . . in the pocketbook."

"Ben," Elizabeth said quickly, "don't buck Sonnerman. You can find another place. Think of the people you can hurt."

His expression was baffled, and a little disappointed. "I put three years of sweat and starvation into that place, Elizabeth. You want me to just walk away from it?"

"You've been paid for your time," she said. "For three years you've been carried on Anse Sonnerman's payroll and drew rations from his cook shack. You can't have your cake and eat it too, Ben."

He became angry. Bright spots of color appeared in his cheeks and his lips pulled into a thin line. Digging into his Mackinaw pocket, he brought out a small flour sack and slammed it down on the table where it clanked loudly. "There's Anse Sonnerman's wages, every dime he paid me in three years. And I've put back the money he spent for grub, too, as near as I can figure it. You still think I ought to walk away from the place?"

Dave Wyatt looked at the sack of money. "There's a goodly amount there," he said.

"I reckon eight hundred dollars," Ben said. He hefted it and stuffed it back in his pocket. "Thanks for the breakfast, but I'm goin' through with what I started."

He turned to the door and Elizabeth followed him outside. She took his arm and pulled him around to face her. "Ben, we know each other well so there shouldn't be any need to pretend. If you stir up anything, Father'll have to go against you, and I don't want that. You do like me, don't you, Ben?"

"Sure, I . . ."

"Then why is it you've never shown me?"

"Well, I . . ."

"You're not a bashful man, are you, Ben?"

He shrugged, and Elizabeth Wyatt stepped close to him, her arms sliding around his waist beneath his coat. For a moment, he waited, then the heat of her body prompted him to put his arms around her. That she wanted his kiss came as a shock to him for she had never exhibited any more than friendliness. Her face was lifted and he kissed her, clumsily at first, then the moist softness of her lips got through to him and the gentleness was forgotten. Perhaps he hurt her; she moaned slightly and clung to him. Then he released her, and she laid her head against his chest.

"Ben, don't spoil this now. I'd come to you, Ben. When I go to town, I could stop."

"I . . . I got to go," he said, and turned away from her, mounting quickly. She came around and reached up for him as if to hold him.

"Ben, think now. Think hard. You could live here." A warm brightness came into her eyes and her voice softened. "You wouldn't regret that, Ben." She stood with her hands behind her, smiling, inviting him to stay.

"I'll see you, Elizabeth," he said, and rode rapidly toward the main road leading down toward the big valley.

As he gained the valley floor, Ben could see other riders in the distance, all heading for Sonnerman's place, as this was the day of reckoning. The day when the men who had proved up would sign over their deeds, take the small bonus, and go back on the old man's payroll as forty a month cowpunchers. Only he wasn't going back; he could not recall exactly when this decision had crystallized, but he had decided.

A dozen ponies stood three-footed before Sonnerman's long porch when Ben Dembrow rode into the yard and dismounted. He stepped across the porch and went in without knocking, for the door was open and the sound of laughter came from the huge parlor. A roaring fire was kicking out heat from the fireplace and Anse Sonnerman stood near it, passing out cigars and free drinks to men he would normally have never allowed inside his house.

Sonnerman was a big man, over six two, and age hadn't softened him much. His hair was as gray as a Montana blizzard and his eyes were like drill points. He had a booming laugh and now it filled the room, for this was his day. At the end of it he'd be richer by twenty some sections of land, which was enough to make any cattleman smile.

Ben Dembrow didn't go into the parlor. Instead, he walked down the long hall to the kitchen and there helped himself to a cup of coffee. While he stood by the stove, cup cradled between his hands, someone came down the hall. He looked around, and then smiled as Enid Sonnerman stepped into the kitchen.

"I saw you ride up," she said. "My window overlooks the yard." She came close and sniffed the cup. "That smells good," she said, and took a sip. Her father's laugh reached a sudden high pitch and Enid whipped her head around. "The bear's really howling today. Did you come over to add your contribution to the pile?"

Somehow she seemed disturbed, which puzzled Ben. He looked at his coffee, then said: "I've decided to keep my place, Enid."

"You haven't!" She sounded shocked and glad and surprised. Ben looked squarely at her. She wasn't as pretty as Elizabeth Wyatt. Enid Sonnerman had a pleasant, smiling face, for she lived with a lot of happiness within her. Her hair was pale wheat and her eyes were almost silver-gray. She was small-boned and her body had gentle curves to it.

"You're mad at me?" Ben asked.

"Ben, I could kiss you." She clasped her hands together. "Do you really mean it? Are you going to stand up to him, Ben?"

"Yep," he said, putting his coffee cup aside. "And the time's here to do it."

He took a step past her, but she put both hands on his chest. "Ben, he's not really a mean man. He's just got an obsession about land." She looked steadily at him. "He'll be wild, Ben. And he'll fight you."

"I know that," Ben Dembrow said. "I left my gun at home, Enid."

"Thank you, Ben."

He looked at her, puzzled. "I thought you'd be mad, Enid. After all, he's your father."

"That's why I'm glad," she said. "I wish more would tell him to go to the devil. Ben, he's wrong. The day's past when one man can own a whole county. But he can't see that, which is too bad."

Anse Sonnerman was bellowing in the parlor and Ben went quickly down the hall. Sonnerman had dragged a table around and was seated before it, money arrayed in neat piles, pen and ink handy for the signing over of the deeds. He had a list of names and began calling them as Ben eased into the room.

Ben nodded to several of the men, then worked his way around toward the east wall. At the end of Sonnerman's long table sat his oldest daughter, Joyce, and to her Ben Dembrow's eyes gravitated. Most men's eyes did, for she was a striking woman. Tall, full-bodied, somewhere in her late twenties, which was an age that appealed to most men, as she retained much of her youthful manner and yet carried an air of knowledge and assurance that can only be found in a woman of experience.

Joyce had the same pale hair that her sister had, but there the resemblance ended. Everyone within thirty miles knew Joyce Sonnerman, and some said that she ran the ranch instead of her father. Ben Dembrow guessed that there was some truth in that. The old man seemed to favor her and broke his back to get her what she wanted.

Anse Sonnerman banged on the table for a little quiet. The talking stopped. He stood up and said: "Seems that you're all here, so we'll get on with our business. Three years ago I gave you all a parcel of land and told you to homestead it." He paused and looked around the room with his sharp eyes. "Now I'm ready to buy it back. Step right up with your paper and we'll get this over with."

Some of the men, Ben noticed, were pretty eager to sign. They crowded around the table. Ben stood back until over half of them went out, the $200 bonus in their pocket and the driving urge to get to town. Ben stepped up to the table.

Sonnerman raised his head. "Been keeping to yourself lately, ain't you, Ben?"

"Pretty much," Ben agreed.

Sonnerman exhibited his eagerness to get on with the business. "You got your deed, Ben?"

"I left it at home," Ben Dembrow said.

This wove a frown of annoyance on Anse Sonnerman's forehead. The others in the room looked solemn-faced and Joyce Sonnerman's expression sharpened. "What is this, Ben?" Sonnerman asked. There was an ominous note in his voice.

"I like my place," Ben said. "And since it's mine, I think I'll keep it."

"That wasn't our deal," Sonnerman declared. He sounded like a man determined not to lose his temper.

"We didn't have a deal," Ben said flatly. "None of us had. You just called us to the house three years ago and told us what you wanted. And we did it. I don't remember any of us promising a danged thing."

Sonnerman said ominously: "You took my wages and now you owe me that land."

"You can have your wages back," Ben said, reaching into his Mackinaw pocket. His hand encountered nothing except some tobacco crumbs and balled lint. Then he began frantically to dig in the other pockets. When he looked at Sonnerman, his face was blank and his manner confused. "I had it when I left home. Over eight hundred dollars. Meant to give it to you." He looked around quickly. "Must have dropped it on the way over. I'll go look for it."

He turned to the door, and Anse Sonnerman said: "Hold that man!"

Several men grabbed Ben Dembrow and he began to fight them. One man hit him savagely behind the ear, and the strength left Ben with a rush. They dragged him back to face Anse Sonnerman, who looked at the young man without a hint of pity.

"You tried to skin me, boy. I take that from no man."

Ben shouted: "You'll get your wages back and more!"

"That's neither here nor there," Sonnerman said. He lowered his voice. "Ben, either you come back today with that deed, or I'll be riding your way in the morning."

"Then you come ahead," Ben Dembrow said flatly.

Sonnerman nodded to the men pinning Ben's arms. "Turn the pup loose." He looked squarely at Ben. "You're sure asking for trouble."

Ben said: "I put my back into buildin' my place and I'm not lettin' it go."

"That's your tough luck. You always did have

big ideas. Now get out . . . and you'd better come back."

Ben looked at Anse Sonnerman, then at Joyce. She was watching him steadily and he found no anger in her eyes. Instead, she seemed amused by this display of mutiny.

He turned away and went outside to his horse.

Enid was on the porch. She looked briefly at Ben and her glance was without much hope. "I heard it all, Ben. And I'm sorry."

"So am I, but I can't back down."

"Then don't." She looked toward the house. "One more thing, Ben. Don't go anywhere without your gun from now on."

"Hell. . . ."

"Ben, I'm telling you, so listen to me!" She whirled then, and went into the house, letting the door slam. He sat his horse for a moment, then rode out of the yard, toward his own place at the foot of the pass.

II

At the age of ten, Ben Dembrow could track game as well as a professional hunter, and during the late morning he summoned all his skill to follow every step he had taken, trying to recover the sack of money he had dropped. The sack had been well tied and the coins in the bottom, amounting to about $100 in gold pieces, would give the whole thing enough weight to keep it from blowing away.

The wind was up, a jerky breeze alternating from nothing to gusts up to twenty miles an hour. The brush was bent each time it tore down off the High Yellows, and the grass cried as he moved along, head down, studying the ground. He did not bother to go back to his own place, but cut around it, driving up the pass road toward Dave Wyatt's small spread.

By the time Ben Dembrow topped the road and turned off toward Wyatt's place, he was dead certain that the money hadn't fallen out of his coat pocket. Which left only one possibility, that he had absent-mindedly left it at Wyatt's place. In which case, it would still be there. Yet he remembered putting it in his coat pocket before leaving.

Wyatt was puttering around the barn when Ben Dembrow came into the yard and dismounted. Elizabeth came to the door and smiled. "Come in, Ben. That wind's cold." He stepped past her, and, before she closed the door, she waved to her father and he came toward the house.

Ben crowded the stove to thaw. "Be snowing by midnight," he said.

Elizabeth poured a cup of coffee and handed it to him. "How did it go, Ben? I don't think I have to ask whether you told him or not."

"I told him, all right," Ben said. He looked

around as Dave Wyatt came in, shutting the door quickly to keep out the wind. "He gave me until tonight to bring him the deed."

"Then you'd better do it," Elizabeth said. "Ben, why do you want to start a war?"

"I don't," he said. "I'm just tired of being a little man. Never enough money to last from year to year. Always scrimpin' and pinchin' to make even my tobacco come out." He looked at Dave Wyatt, who was shucking out of his coat. "You know how I feel, Dave."

Wyatt sighed. "Yes, I know. Been that way all my life. If I haven't been working for another fella, I've been grubbing it out on some place like this. A man needs money to make money, Ben."

"Speaking of money," Ben Dembrow said, "I lost that sack I had this morning."

"Lost it?" Dave Wyatt acted as though he couldn't believe it. "How could you lose that much money, Ben?"

"It was gone when I reached into my pocket," he said. "I've backtracked, but I can't find it."

"You didn't leave it here," Elizabeth said quickly. "I saw you put it in your pocket."

"A thing like that weighs," Dave Wyatt said, as though he hadn't heard Elizabeth. "Ben, how could a thing like that drop out without your noticin' it?"

"You get used to carryin' a weight around," Ben said. "Hell, I lost my gun once and never knowed it until that same night." He sipped his coffee and worry wove lines in his forehead. "Made me out a damned fool in front of Sonnerman. Especially after I bragged that I was goin' to pay him back every cent."

Elizabeth frowned. "Ben, I told you." She shrugged. "What's the use. You're too stubborn to listen to anyone."

Her father asked: "You goin' home, Ben?"

"Why, sure. I got my horse herd to look after."

"But ain't Sonnerman goin' to . . . ?"

"He's going to try," Ben said, grinning.

"Hate to see that, boy. When bullets start flyin', no man's safe." He squinted at Ben Dembrow. "Sorry about your money. Know you scrimped to save it. The temptation must have been mighty great to spend it." He looked a little dreamy-eyed. "Don't know when I've seen that much money at one time. Was I that well off, I'd buy me a new buggy. Ride to town in style. Might even buy a store derby hat. And a cigar on Saturday night."

"Well," Ben Dembrow said, "I got to get along. If you hear of anyone finding that money, you'll let me know, won't you?"

"Of course," Dave Wyatt said. "We're honest folk, Ben. Thought you knew that."

"Sure, sure," Ben said, opening the door. "Good bye, Elizabeth."

She looked at him, a brightness in her eyes too

plain to be misunderstood. "Good bye?" Her laugh was soft and reminding. "Ben, never good bye."

Dave Wyatt walked with Dembrow, and stood there while he mounted. "Ben, my little girl gets mighty lonely up here, nearest neighbor bein' six miles west. And loneliness festers up a heap of foolish notions, especially about men. Wouldn't want to see her hurt, Ben."

"You can say it plainer than that, Dave."

"Guess I can," Wyatt admitted. "With this trouble comin' up between you and Sonnerman, I don't think you ought to come around to see Elizabeth. At least until it blows over."

Ben chuckled. "A month ago you was all for me marryin' her."

"Well, things change," Wyatt said. "No offense, Ben, but you ain't such a good catch now."

"Thanks for telling me," Ben said, and spurred his horse out of the yard. Ben was more concerned over money than Wyatt's opinion of him as a son-in-law. Ben felt morally obligated to pay Sonnerman back, every cent. That meant selling the horses; there was no other way.

At his home place, Ben cooked a hurried meal. Although it was late afternoon, he saddled a fresh horse and started for Rimrock, eight miles away. Money became a horrible word to Ben Dembrow and he dreaded selling off his stock. The profit to be made would hinge on his being able to hold onto them until spring; the ranches always bought their saddle stock then.

He tried to figure what kind of a price he'd get and couldn't; his only chance of breaking even lay in getting to town before Sonnerman sent in the word of what happened. Any horse trader was in business to make money, and, if they discovered that Ben was against the wall, the price would go to rock bottom.

Rimrock wasn't much in size. Three streets in each direction, all flanked by homes or stores, Rimrock sat against the east end of the valley with mountains beginning less than a mile beyond. The wind tore down the main drag, flapping signs, making men walk along head down, one hand on their hat brims.

Ben Dembrow went to the east end of the main street, then turned off on a short side alley until he came to Wilkerson's Stable and Livery Barn. Wilkerson was a prune of a man, sixty if he was a day, and as sharp a horse trader as ever set foot in Montana. He squinted at Ben as he dismounted, then followed him to the two-by-four shack that Wilkerson used for an office. The boards closed out some of the chill wind and Ben got right down to business.

"Want to sell off," he said.

"Everything?" When Ben nodded, Wilkerson scratched his whiskered cheek. "Have to hand feed until spring. Market's down. Couldn't ship

East. Ain't anybody buying around here, Ben."

"How much?"

"Bein' it's you and I know you're honest, thirty-five a head."

Ben Dembrow couldn't believe it. "Hell, I've been all summer breaking those ponies for saddle stock. A scrub mustang is worth fifty unbroken!"

"True," Wilkerson admitted. "Still, thirty-five's my best offer. I made it right off, knowing you wasn't in a mood to dicker."

"What makes you think . . . ?" Ben stopped, and went out into the stable. He looked around and found what he was looking for, horses with the Sonnerman brand on their flanks.

Wilkerson followed him and leaned back against a stall, a slight smile on his face. "Ringo came in an hour ago. Sorry, Ben, the word's out. I couldn't buy your stock unless I stole 'em. Sonnerman would run me out of town if I offered you a cent more."

"I didn't know you kissed his feet," Ben said angrily.

"Son, we always kiss the feet of those that have money."

Ben went to his pony, vaulting into the saddle. He turned west on the main drag until he came to Hunter's Store, then dismounted, and went inside. Several town ladies were chattering over some new dress goods just in from St. Louis. Ben went on back to where Hunter waited at the grocery counter. The store was warm, made so by a glowing pot-bellied stove, and the aroma of leather mingled with sacked coffee and spices and dried fruit.

Jim Hunter was a man in his thirties, hiding himself behind thick glasses and an inscrutable manner. He nodded politely to Ben, then said: "I'll save you the trouble and embarrassment, Ben. Ringo spread the word. Your credit's been cut off at the pockets."

The anger, when it came, was sudden and almost killing in intensity. Ben fisted a handful of Hunter's shirt and nearly hauled him over the counter. Yet Hunter's face never changed; he was as calm as a man playing whist. "You going to hit me, Ben? Will that solve anything?"

Ben Dembrow let him go, and then stood there, wiping his hands on his Mackinaw. "Sorry, Jim. I just wanted to hit something." He paused to take a deep breath. "I've got four dollars. That ought to buy something."

"Not in this store," Hunter said softly. "Ben, there isn't a merchant in town that will sell to you."

"I see," Ben said. "That's the way Sonnerman would have to play it. The sheriff couldn't throw me off my own place, and Sonnerman wouldn't dare burn me out without going to jail."

"It's tough," Jim Hunter admitted. "And it's tough on me to say no. But I have to carry the farmers all winter on credit, just the same as everybody in Rimrock. Sonnerman has money because he sells off in the fall. If I didn't have his business, I couldn't pay my bills, Ben."

"Yeah, yeah," Ben said, not wanting to hear anyone else's troubles when he had so many of his own. He turned and stalked out of Hunter's, turning right toward the saloon on the corner.

For a moment he felt a little panic as though he were locked in a room with walls, ceiling, and floor all coming together at the same time. He pushed into the saloon and looked around. A few townsmen sat at the back tables, playing cards, while two men stood at the bar, glasses in hand. And just the two men he wanted to see.

Dan Ringo turned when Ben's elbow gouged him in the ribs. "You're really looking for trouble, ain't you, Ben?"

"Yep," Ben said. He spun $1 on the bar and waited while the bartender looked at it. "Whiskey."

The bartender licked his lips and glanced at Dan Ringo. The man next to Ringo moved away, thereby declaring that he was out of this. Ben knew him, had ridden with him, and knew him to be a quiet cowpuncher, not given to trouble.

Ringo looked at the money on the bar. "That's no good in Rimrock. Might as well throw it away."

To prove it, he picked up the dollar and dropped it in the filthy spittoon. Ben looked down at the molasses-thick juice that was a blend of tobacco and anyone's guess what else. Then he looked at Ringo. "You mind picking that out of there now?" he asked.

Ringo tipped his head back and laughed, a mistake if he ever made one, because while the point of his jaw was exposed, Ben Dembrow nailed it with his fist. The power of the punch drove Ringo back. He went into the table where the three men played cards, scattering them and the game over the south end of the saloon.

He struck and rolled, losing his gun, which was a good thing because he went for it as soon as enough sense returned to know what he was doing.

Ben left the bar and walked over as Ringo got to his feet. Ben's boot sent the .44 scooting out of reach, and then he met Ringo's bull charge.

They collided and Ben gave ground, his feet trampling the sawdust. Ringo was trying to butt with his head, but Ben kept hacking at him with short, driving punches, upsetting him, jarring him badly.

The three townsmen found the fight more interesting than their card game and righted table and chairs to watch in comfort. Ringo was trying to hang on to Ben while some of the giddiness left him.

But Ben wouldn't have that at all. He was willing to take a fist across the mouth to get in a good lick of his own and he kept backing away from Ringo, and belting him every time an opening showed itself.

Above the push and sigh of the wind could be heard their breathing and the meaty smack of fists against flesh. Ben was bleeding from the nose and Ringo had a long cut over his eye. Ringo tried to square off and nail Ben, but the punch was wild and Ringo nearly upset himself.

Ben laced him into the stomach with an axe blow and Ringo's cry was a deep wheeze low in his throat. His eyes turned to glass and Ben straightened him with an uppercut that began around his knees. Ringo went back into the bar, rapping it solidly, and Ben followed him. His fists sounded like a butcher flopping meat on the chopping block. Ringo would have fallen had not Ben held him with one hand.

The front door opened and slammed, and then a deep voice said: "He's had enough, Ben!"

With dream slowness, Ben looked around and saw Sheriff Arly Burke standing there, legs widespread, authority in every feature. Nodding, Ben pulled Ringo away from the bar and flung him to the floor, where he braced himself on hands and knees.

"Now fish out that dollar," Ben ordered, between ragged sawings for wind.

Ringo just hung his head and sobbed.

Ben said: "Dan, I can give you some more. You want that?"

215

Ringo managed to shake his head.

"Then pick out that dollar," Ben said.

The sheriff came up to the bar and looked on, puzzled. He opened his mouth to speak, then thought better of it, closing it with a snap.

Slowly Dan Ringo crawled to the spittoon and hesitatingly put his hand in deep. He had to dig around a bit before he found the dollar. But he got it.

"Get up." Ben's voice was hard. Ringo knew when he had been ridden down and did as he was told, not looking at Ben Dembrow. "Now put it on the bar and order me a drink," Ben said.

There was a limit to what a man would take, but Ringo no longer cared. He had dipped his hand into a spittoon to do another man's bidding, which finished him on this range. The next time he gave an order it would likely be thrown back in his teeth.

"Give . . . give him a drink," Ringo said to the bartender.

"Now crawl out of here," Ben ordered.

"Let him walk," the sheriff said softly.

"I said he crawls!" Ben glared at Arly Burke, but the sheriff's glance was as mild and pleasant as a man's could be. Only Ben Dembrow wasn't fooled a bit. Burke had handled men as tough as they grew and some said his draw was second only to Wyatt Earp's.

"He's had enough," Arly Burke said softly. His glance touched the cowpuncher who stood farther down the bar. "If you belong to the Sonnerman brand, get Ringo out of here." When the cowpuncher turned to pick up Dan Ringo's .44, Burke said: "Leave that. He might do something foolish and get killed for it."

With a helping hand, Ringo made the door. Several minutes later the three townsmen left, to spread the word most likely. The bartender had poured Ben's drink and placed his change on the bar.

Sheriff Arly Burke leaned heavily on his forearms and said: "Got you pretty proddy, didn't they, Ben?"

"You expect me to take it on my back?"

"Nope," Burke said softly. "But we have law here, Ben. Best never to forget that."

"I'm not going to," he said, downing his whiskey. "Better see that Anse Sonnerman don't, either."

"I'll tell him where he stands," Burke said. "The first man who starts the shooting is going to end up in jail. I mean it, Ben."

"I know you do."

Burke sighed. "By rights, I could lock you up for fighting in town and disturbing the peace." He smiled. "But you've got enough trouble now, Ben. And Ringo had that coming. The man has a heavy hand that irks the hell out of me."

"Thanks," Ben Dembrow said. "I sure lost my temper."

"If you intend to do that often, better make it a habit not to wear a gun." He turned around and hooked his elbows on the bar edge. "What're you going to do, Ben? Can you last the winter?"

"I don't know. Credit's been cut off."

"A dirty way to fight," Burke agreed. "But I can't do a thing to stop it." He grinned and put his hand briefly on Ben Dembrow's shoulder. "Stay with it, kid. You may run the old man into his hole yet. Been a long time coming. But remember what I said. The first man who puts a bullet in somebody is in trouble. I'd come after you, Ben. Wouldn't like it, but I would."

Burke turned then, and walked out. Wind howled through the open door for a brief instant, then was closed out as it was pulled shut. Ben stood at the bar, his empty shot glass in front of him. Finally he said: "Can I wash in your back room, Harry?"

"Sure, Ben. Help yourself." Dembrow walked toward the side door and stopped there when the bartender said: "You goin' back home, Ben?"

"What else is there?"

The bartender frowned. "You believe the sheriff, about coming after you if you start shooting?"

"Sure. Why?"

The bartender shrugged. "Nothing, I guess. Only it just occurred to me that maybe Sonnerman won't."

III

That evening Ben Dembrow made a slow ride toward his own place; he was too stiff and sore from his set-to with Dan Ringo to make better time. And there was that change in the weather that he had prophesied. Around eight the wind petered out to a faint breeze and a short time later the snow began to fall, gently at first, then heavier until the night seemed filled with swirling bits of cotton.

By ten o'clock he was riding by feel for the road was obscured by a thick blanket of snow, and around eleven he bumped into the southeast corner of his huge corral. Following this around, he went on to the barn and there put up his horse. On the back porch he paused to stomp the snow from his boots, and then stepped inside.

Immediately he whirled, for the stove was simmering and a blast of warm air struck him squarely. He was halfway through the door on his way out when Enid Sonnerman's voice said: "Ben!"

He stopped, feeling pretty foolish. "Light a lamp," he said, and came back in, closing the door.

She moved about in the darkness, cracked herself against the table edge, and swore politely. Then she found the lamp and put a match to the

wick. A warm glow began to invade the blackness, spreading until only the corners remained
gloomy. Ben Dembrow took off his coat and
shook the snow from it.

When Enid saw the marks on his face, she said:
"Ringo looks a lot worse." She giggled. "Father
was foaming at the mouth, Ben. He fired Ringo
on the spot."

Ben looked steadily at Enid Sonnerman. "What
are you doing here, Enid?"

"I heard that Father cut you off at the pockets
in town, so I brought over a buckboard full of
supplies." She smiled. "Enough to last you over
the winter."

He shook his head. "Why should you go against
him, Enid?"

"To help him," she said. She read his frown
correctly and explained. "Ben, by helping you,
I'm doing him a big favor. He's had his way
too long, Ben. Walked over people so much
he thinks anybody else's opinion isn't worth
listening to. He needs a good fight. Not where
he'll really get hurt, but enough of one to show
him that he can't run everybody."

Ben laughed softly. "You're quite a girl, Enid."

"I didn't think you'd noticed," she said. "I'll
make some coffee."

He sat at the table while she sifted grounds into
the pot, then went to the door and dumped them
out. Instantly he was on his feet, shouting: "What

did you do that for? Holy smoke, you ruined the coffee! Take me a week to build up another pot of grounds like that."

"I'm doing this," she said firmly. "Better get used to it."

Somewhere along the track of his life he had gleaned that bit of wisdom that told him never to argue with a woman. He sat at the table while she made the coffee her way. While the pot rocked and thumped on the stove, she sat down across from him.

"Did you find the money, Ben?"

He looked at her sharply. "I thought no one believed me."

"I believed you. And I think Father did, too."

"The money just disappeared," Ben said. "I went over every inch of the ground. Didn't see any other tracks where someone could have picked it up, either. Sure is strange."

Outside, the wind picked up, slamming against the cabin. Ben got up and opened the door and was immediately pushed back a step. The snow fell even thicker, driven now by a singing wind. He closed the door and came back to the table. "Reg'lar blue norther out there. Better get you home pretty quick. The temperature's dropped and that stuff will drift into windrows in an hour or so."

"There's plenty of time." She got up to take the coffee off the stove, and, when she sat down again, each had a steaming cup. "Ben, where are you from? I mean, before you came here to work for Father?"

He shrugged. "Kansas. No folks. Been on my own so long now I can't remember a time when I wasn't." He fell silent for a moment. "Maybe that's why this place means so much to me."

While she thoughtfully finished the cup, he got an extra muffler and shirt, donning these hurriedly. The wind was strong, and, when they went out, it shoved at them, forcing them to walk head down and leaning slightly forward. Ben left the lamp on in the cabin to act as a beacon for finding his way back.

He saddled a fresh horse and brought him around to the sheltered side where Enid waited with the buckboard. Ben tied his saddle horse to the back and got in, taking the reins from her. The snow was piling now and he had to bear dead against the storm. With the temperature dropped five degrees, the snow was a nettle stinging against his face.

She sat beside him, bundled in her coat, a scarf around her head and face. There was no talk between them. The wind tore around them, a driving power that kept making the horses turn away from it. Ben watched the team carefully, pulling back every time they wanted to swing.

They met cattle lowing and drifting before the storm and twice were stalled by a huge windrow that forced Ben to dismount and scout out a passage that was less deep. Already a nagging doubt was building in his mind and after an hour of this he judged that he had traveled less than a mile and a half. He came back, took the team in hand, and turned them, putting the storm at his back. Then he got in the rig and tried to follow his own trail.

Enid kept looking at him, but said nothing. For a time Ben could make out his trail, but the wind soon smoothed it over and the last mile he navigated purely by feel. Even then he was off, for Enid saw the light away off to the right and grabbed his arm.

Ben could not recall when anything looked so good as that lamp burning. He quartered the team to the storm, realizing then that he had been thrown off when the wind shifted a little on him. The team was tired to the point of stopping in their tracks and Ben had to drive them the rest of the way. Pulling close to the barn, he got down to fight open the door, then drove team and buckboard inside. Enid sat on the seat, teeth chattering while Ben unharnessed and put up his own horse.

Then they crossed to the cabin. The fire was down and Ben hastily stoked it. "Get those clothes dry," he said. "Don't let the snow melt on them."

He shed his own coat, dropping it on the floor

in his haste to get heat into the place. Enid backed against the stove as it began to throw out a new heat. Ben took her coat and his own and hung them up.

"Looks like you won't go any place tonight," he said. "Sorry, Enid."

"Couldn't be helped," she said. "Joyce won't miss me until morning anyway." She looked around the room at the meager possessions of Ben Dembrow. His bed sat in one corner, home-made, as was the other furniture.

He guessed her thoughts and said: "I'll sleep in front of the fire. You better get out of those things and get 'em dried out. The hem of your dress is soaked. Probably your shoes are, too."

She hesitated a moment, then pulled a chair around in front of the fire and unlaced her high shoes. He took a spare blanket from the closet and handed it to her, then stood with his back turned while she shed her dress and four petticoats.

Ben had an old lariat strung from wall to wall. After a moment's embarrassed hesitation, she hung these delicate items to dry. Moving around in a thin, cotton chemise, especially with a man in the room, made her nervous and she quickly draped the blanket around her. The rough wool scratched her bare shoulders and legs.

"You can turn around now," she said softly.

He made a deliberate effort to ignore the underclothes hanging on the rope, but this was nearly impossible as he bumped them every time he crossed the room. The wind battered at the cabin with furious force, and he stepped outside a moment to bring in more firewood, enough to last out the night. Enid sat on the chair before the fire, staring at the flickering light.

Ben said: "After you get in bed, I'll need that blanket."

"All right."

He heated two bricks and placed them between the blankets near the foot, and then turned his back while she got into bed. Enid pulled the blankets to her chin and watched him as he snuffed out the lamp, then sat down in front of the fire. He took off his shirt, which was wet from snow drifting down the collar, and spread it to dry. Then he wrestled with his boots and soaked socks.

Finally Ben said: "I sure don't relish facin' your dad now. This ain't going to be easy to explain, let alone expect him to believe."

"He'll just have to believe it," Enid said. "He doesn't have any choice."

Settling on the hard floor, Ben Dembrow kept thinking about the girl across the room. Impulse was strong in him, yet he held back, swayed by some misplaced sense of chivalry. He slept in snatches, waking when the room began to get cold. Hour by hour the night wore away, and, when he judged the time to be near dawn, he got up and put on his dry shirt. A look outside convinced him that the storm had blown itself out. Along his west fence, Sonnerman's cattle were bunched in misery, kept from the pass by the stout fence.

Then Ben saw the riders, four of them, working through the cattle, coming toward his place. In the cold air, voices traveled a great distance and he went back inside to get his coat. He chose an inopportune time to reënter the cabin. Enid was standing in the middle of the room, clad only in her shift. She looked startled for an instant, then tried to cover her bare legs and shoulders at the same time, neither successfully.

"No time for modesty," Ben said flatly. "Your father's coming and he has friends with him."

"Oh!" she said, and began to put on her petti-coats, paying no attention to Ben. Shrugging into his Mackinaw, Ben stepped outside as Anse Sonnerman came around the end of the huge corral. Joyce was with him, plus two of their hands.

The old man was wrapped to the nose in a heavy muffler, and, when he spoke, his voice sounded like the echo from a cavern. "I'm looking for my youngest, Dembrow."

"She's here," Ben said easily. "The storm came up and I couldn't get her home."

"I won't ask how hard you tried," Sonnerman said. He motioned for Joyce to get down.

Joyce went inside quickly. "Enid! Oh, this is simply disgraceful!"

"Mister Sonnerman," Ben said, "no harm would ever come to her here."

The old man's face was carved from granite. "There's only one honorable answer for this, Dembrow. But the thought of it chokes me."

". . . But Joyce, I tell you, nothing . . ."

"No need to get your back humped," Ben said quickly. "She slept in the bed and I slept on the floor, if that's what's worryin you."

"We'll not discuss it here," Sonnerman said flatly.

". . . Then you're a fool, Enid! A miserable little fool! You could have put him in the palm of Papa's hand. . . ."

"I expected you back yesterday," Sonnerman said. "I'll take the deed now, Dembrow."

"You'll have to take it all right," Ben said. "Because I sure won't hand it to you."

Enid came out then, Joyce behind her. Sonnerman speared Enid with his sharp eyes. "You've brought disgrace on me, Enid. There's only one way out."

"You're being ridiculous . . . ," she began, but her father cut her off.

"Enough! Get on with Joyce!" He looked at Ben Dembrow. "The wedding will be in town tomorrow at eleven o'clock. Don't miss it."

"Now wait. . . ."

"Waiting's over!" Sonnerman snapped. "Dembrow, Arly Burke warned me not to lay a finger on you. I'll not step outside the law to get a man like you. I'll not need to now. After the weddin', we'll talk about tearing down this fence to let my cattle through. I'll give you a just price for your horses and then you can work for me. There's always room for another foreman on my place. . . ."

Ben Dembrow shouted: "Get the hell off my property!"

Anse Sonnerman leaned forward and spoke with rigid control. "Eleven tomorrow, Dembrow."

He wheeled his horse, and the others followed, pushing and driving through the white drifts. Ben Dembrow stood there and watched them leave. Before they pulled out of sight, Enid turned in the saddle and looked back at him, but the distance was too great to read her expression.

IV

Ben Dembrow had his morning chores to do, and it was a little after one o'clock before he finished with them. It was then that he saw two riders coming down the pass road and recognized Dave Wyatt and his daughter Elizabeth. They came on steadily and Ben waited until they swung into his yard.

"There's coffee on," he said, moving around to help Elizabeth down. Dave went on into the cabin. Ben followed with Elizabeth. He closed the door to keep out the cold, and the Wyatts gathered around the stove.

Ben said: "Sonnerman was here a while ago."

"You still holdin' out?"

"Yes."

"Hmmm," Wyatt said. "Talked to some of the folks in the Yellows since I seen you last."

"So?"

"They're a solid mind not to get mixed up in this, Ben."

"Nobody asked them to."

Wyatt's eyebrows raised slightly. "You don't seem to understand, boy. We got to do business with Sonnerman to stay alive. Can't do business with him and stay friendly with you at the same time."

Ben asked softly: "You closing me out, Dave?"

"Ben," Elizabeth said quickly, "we don't want to."

"But not very hard," he said.

She came up to him and put her hand on his arm. "Ben, try to understand, we're just little people. We can't fight Sonnerman and win."

Ben rubbed his jaw. "I was about to ask you if you could spare a few ton of hay to carry me through."

Wyatt shook his head sadly. "Turning you down

is hard, Ben, but I got no choice. Was Sonnerman to find out I sold you hay, he'd never buy from me again." His voice pleaded: "Patch this up, boy, before a lot of innocent people get hurt."

"Innocent?" Ben looked oddly at Dave Wyatt. "Why innocent, Dave? I've sat at your table plenty of times and listened to you talk of the day when Sonnerman would be against the wall . . . and you'd be down in the valley gobblin' up the best sections of land."

"Just talk," Wyatt said quickly. He looked at Elizabeth. "We got to be goin', Ben. Thought we'd go into town. Do a little shoppin'." He laughed softly and rubbed his hands together. "A man's got to get away from his labor once in a while." He stepped outside.

Elizabeth lingered a moment, then said: "Ben, I'm not against you. Do you believe me?"

"I don't know what to believe, Elizabeth."

She stepped close and quickly kissed him. "Would I do that if I didn't . . . if I weren't fond of you? Ben, can you forget the way we were the other night?"

He looked at her carefully. "What are you getting at?"

"There'll be other times like that." She squeezed his arm. "Pa'll be waiting. I have to go. But I'll be back, Ben."

He stood in the doorway and watched her leave. Her father was mounted and impatient to get started, and they rode out as soon as Elizabeth mounted.

Ben Dembrow smiled to himself. There was a fire in Elizabeth Wyatt that ate at him, pushed exciting thoughts into his mind. That Elizabeth was a woman! Nothing wishy-washy about her. Had Elizabeth been in Enid's place during the storm—Ben smiled again.

Going to the barn, he saddled his best horse and flipped into the saddle, turning toward the Rimrock road. The going was slow, and he arrived in Rimrock in mid-afternoon.

He put up his horse at the stable and walked along the main drag. Most of the businessmen had their boardwalks shoveled and he looked in three or four of the stores, then decided to see if Arly Burke was at his office on the side street.

The front door was unlocked and Ben let himself in. A pot-bellied stove in the corner pushed heat into the room. Ben heard Burke in the cell-blocks, talking to one of the prisoners. Burke came out a few minutes later and seemed surprised to find Ben Dembrow sitting by the desk.

He hung up his keys and peeled a wrapper from a cigar. "Troubles, Ben? More, I mean."

"You got no idea," Ben said, and told him the whole story.

Burke listened with patient attention, puffing now and then to send ribbons of smoke past his face. When the story was finished, Burke asked: "How does Enid feel about it?"

"The old man never gave her a chance to say. And that damned Joyce was jumpin' all over her for not doin' what she's accused of. Figured to get me under the old man's thumb that way."

"Looks like he's going to have you there, anyway," Arly Burke said. "You're in trouble, Ben."

"And that's not all." Ben spread his hands. "Hell, it's Elizabeth Wyatt I like!"

"That's a pretty way for the wind to blow," Burke opined. "Are you going to show up in the morning?"

"I'll show," Ben said very quietly.

Arly Burke's eyes narrowed at Ben's soft tone. He didn't like it. Burke paused thoughtfully to shake the ash from his cigar. "Anyway, Enid must feel something toward you or she wouldn't have come over with the grub."

"She's just naturally kind," Ben said. "A man wants more than that in a woman."

Burke put his tongue in his cheek. "Seems that you had a chance to find out and passed it up." He stood up, and crossed to the window to look onto the street. He sighed deeply. "Dan Ringo's in town. Been making a lot of loud talk about you."

"Oh?"

"He feels that he's got a right to square things,"

Burke said. "You pushed his head into the dirt a little too far, Ben."

"I'm not carrying a gun." Ben got up. He went to the door.

Burke said: "Ben, watch yourself from here on in. The blue chips are all in and the hand can get rough."

"Don't I know it," he said, and went out.

He cruised up and down the street for a half hour, then went over to the hotel and took a seat on the porch, a position that gave him a good view of the saloon, which was Dan Ringo's favorite hang-out.

From the east end of the street a new buggy drew Ben Dembrow's attention, then he straightened in his chair as the rig drew nearer and he recognized Dave Wyatt, sitting proud and sassy, a derby cocked rakishly to one side of his head, and a cigar streaming fragrance as he pushed along. Dave Wyatt wheeled by, saw Ben Dembrow, and tipped his hat. Ben left his chair and stepped off the porch as Dave whipped into a U-turn, then came to a halt by the hitch rack.

"Pretty, ain't it?"

"Expensive, too," Ben said. "A rig like that would set a man back seventy-five dollars." He looked carefully at Dave Wyatt. "That a quarter cigar?"

"Have one," Dave Wyatt said, and pulled a half dozen from his inner pocket, offering Dembrow one.

Ben shook his head. "Livin' pretty high on the hog, ain't you, Dave?"

Wyatt frowned as he put the cigars away. "You trying to say somethin', then say it."

"Come into some money sudden like?" Ben asked quietly.

"Ha! Knew that's what it was. Says to Elizabeth . . . 'That Ben'll accuse me the minute I buy a new shirt.'" He shook his finger at Ben Dembrow. "I'm a savin' man. Ask anybody and they'll tell you thrift's my middle name. Coincidence, that's what it is, you losin' your money and me spendin' a bit. Now let's see you argue that."

"Dave, you're as tight as the bark on a sycamore," Ben said. "And a penny-pincher like you don't buy buggies and quarter cigars."

"Hell you say!" Dave Wyatt laughed and thumped his bowler. "You left out the derby." His gaiety vanished and he bent toward Ben Dembrow, his expression severe. "Now I'm going to tell you once, so you listen close. My money's my own, and, if I hear a word about what you think and what I know, I'll have the law on you for slander!"

He straightened on the seat and clucked to his team, wheeling on down the street. Ben watched him, then crossed over, and walked four doors down to the mercantile.

Jim Hunter was in the back room taking inventory when Ben walked through the store.

He looked around, a little surprised to see Dembrow in the middle of the afternoon.

"Talk to you?" Ben asked.

Hunter smiled and put pad and pencil aside. "Talk's free, Ben. What's the subject?"

"Buggies," Ben said. "Just saw Dave Wyatt with a new Studebaker."

"Nice model," Jim Hunter said. "A little gaudy for the conservative businessman, perhaps, but I understand the young bucks in San Francisco really go for 'em." He looked slantways at Ben Dembrow. "You thinking about a new buggy, Ben?"

"Not to buy," Ben said. "I was just wondering about Dave, though. The man never spends a nickel unless he's forced to."

"Well, he paid cash for this," Hunter said. "Cleared up his bill, too. Surprised me a little because it came to over forty dollars. Been carrying him over two months, you know." He wiped a hand across his face. "Ben, I know about you losing the money. Don't put two and two together in public unless you can prove it. A man can be sued, you know, and, if he got judgment, he could take your place."

"Well," Ben said, "thanks anyway, Jim."

The town suddenly left a bad taste in his mouth, but going back to the home place was equally distasteful. He crossed over to the hotel and pressed the clerk for a room. The clerk was about to argue, but the look on Ben Dembrow's face pushed the idea aside. He presented a key, took the dollar, and kept quiet.

With the door locked, Ben Dembrow lay on the bed until dark, then went down the street to a small restaurant for his supper. Afterward, he walked around, feeling time heavy on his hands. Coming out on the main drag, he saw Joyce Sonnerman come into town in a small sleigh. She pulled up in front of Rimrock's two-by-four bank, knocked a moment, then went inside when the owner opened the door. Ben stood in the dark shadow of a building corner and waited. She came out a moment later, stuffing a package in her handbag. Then she crossed to the hotel, after giving one of the town loafers a quarter to take her team and rig to the stable.

Ben clung to his dark retreat for a time, then walked back to the hotel, looking in through the front window before crossing the lobby. The clerk was nodding behind his desk and Ben went up the stairs. As he moved down the lamplit hall, a door opened and Joyce looked out.

"Ben," she said, "will you step in, please?"

She had a way about her that made men do exactly as she wanted, even when they had a mind in the other direction. Before he thought, Ben had his hat off and was standing in her room while she closed the door and turned the key.

"Sit down, Ben," she said coolly. "You're not afraid of me, are you?"

"No," he said, and wondered why it sounded like a lie. She moved about the room and he watched her, and she knew that he watched, just as all men watched, and carried on those small bits of wishful fantasy.

Finally she sat down. She reached over and took his hand. "Poor, confused Ben. I know that you like Enid. Why, you've taken her to dances, and . . ." She leaned forward and her voice was very soft. "What really happened, Ben? You're not really fooling me. Father, perhaps, because he's very idealistic. And I have no doubt at all about Enid."

He gently shook off her hand. "You've got a bad mind, Joyce."

"Really," she said, her voice heavily sarcastic. "I know how the world runs, so don't sit there and act like a fool. Father's got you pressed against the wall and you don't have anything to fight with." She turned and snatched up her handbag, opening it. "Here," she said, waving a packet of bills. "Five hundred dollars. That's fair enough for your place. Take it and get out of the country tonight."

Ben reminded her: "I'm supposed to get married at eleven tomorrow."

"Oh, don't be an utter fool," Joyce said. "The stakes are a lot higher than you think. Ben, I'll level with you. You're just a little man, and the Yellows is full of little men. But you're sitting right in the middle of the pass and we don't like that."

"We?"

"All right, *me* then. You've heard people say that I run the ranch. They're not far off. And what I run, I run hard. I want the farmers out of the Yellows and I mean to get them out of there, but I'll never do it with you sitting there in the pass with your stupid horse ranch." She slapped the money against her palm. "That's a lot, Ben. Keep you going for two years, seeing as how you lay off booze and cards . . . and women, maybe."

"You'd better keep it," Ben said softly. "I don't like the proposition."

"All right," she said without anger. "Perhaps you'll change your mind before eleven tomorrow. But I wouldn't wait too long. Father's going to bring Enid to town at ten. You decide before then."

His eyebrows pulled down and he studied this woman, so beautiful and so very hard. "You know," he said, "you're coasting along on the old man's reputation, Joyce. Is he getting a little tired of riding big? Once he came down off that horse and showed a hole in him, people would start pushing the Sonnermans back, wouldn't they?"

"You're smart," she admitted. "But then I always gave you credit for that. Ben, if you whipped Father in this, he'd never have his say again. Every farmer in the Yellows would jack up the hay price and . . ."

"And you'd have to pay the going market rate instead of a squeeze price." Ben Dembrow picked up his hat and stepped to the door. "Joyce," he said, gaining a sudden insight into this woman, "you ever spent a stormy night alone with a man in a . . . ?"

"Get out!" she shouted.

Ben Dembrow smiled. "Got through to you, didn't I? That shell wasn't as thick as you thought, huh? Sure, I can see why you want to believe bad about Enid. You believe that way because you can see yourself in her place, and we can both guess . . ."

"Who has the bad mind?" she snapped.

Ben turned the key and opened the door a crack. "What do you think about, Joyce? Men? You must be near thirty. . . ."

"If you don't go, I'll call the owner," she said, withdrawing again into her cold shell.

"Go ahead and call him." Ben stepped into the hall. "Better lock this door. . . ."

She threw a full pitcher of water at him, but he slammed the door and heard the pitcher shatter harmlessly.

The lobby was empty when he crossed it and stepped onto the street. He pulled his Mackinaw tighter around his neck for the temperature was down to zero and gusts of wind were whipping dry snow down the street.

The town was a lonely place, with all its people, and because Ben Dembrow felt particularly friendless, he turned onto the side street and walked to the jail. He found Arly Burke at his desk, cleaning the bore of his rifle. Ben closed the door and leaned his shoulders against it.

"More weather in the making," Burke said. He jerked his thumb toward the stove in the corner. "Coffee there. Cups in the cabinet."

Ben crossed over and poured, then stood there with the cup cradled between his hands.

Burke glanced at Dembrow. "Coffee all right? Pretty strong, but that's the way I like it." He *clacked* the action closed on the rifle and placed it in the rack. "Saw Joyce Sonnerman come into town."

"Is there anything you don't see?" Ben asked.

"Not much," Burke admitted. "A man gets the habit of looking and it never leaves him."

"I talked to her at the hotel," Ben said. "She offered me five hundred dollars to leave the country."

Burke whistled softly. "So that's what she went to the bank for." He shook his head. "I can guess what you told her." He flung an arm over the back of his chair and studied Ben Dembrow. "The snow bunch up the old man's cattle near your fence?"

"Yeah," Ben said. "Tough on the cattle."

"Cut a hole in the fence and let 'em through," Burke suggested mildly.

"Sure," said Ben. "And take the chance of my horses drifting. That's sure likely."

Burke pointed out: "Cold snap might come up, say twenty below, and the cattle would freeze standing up. A sight like that could drive Sonnerman to kill."

Ben drained his coffee and put the cup aside. "Anse would cut the fence before that happened."

"Then I'd have to arrest him," Burke said. "Would you let him cut it, Ben? That fence is your property, you know, and, if a man tried to destroy it, you could put a bullet in him and the law could never touch you."

Ben buttoned his Mackinaw. "I could do that, couldn't I?"

V

Ben Dembrow made a night ride to his home place to check his stock and afterward turned into a cold bed and spent a restless night. The next morning he woke at daybreak and, after breakfast, went to the barn for his horse. The day was gray and windy and the promise of more foul weather was plain enough to the man who could read the signs.

Ben looked at his fence where Sonnerman's cattle bunched, then turned his horse toward Rimrock.

When he stabled his horse and walked along Rimrock's main street, he felt that the news was out about the shotgun wedding; men looked at each other and smiled knowingly.

Ben went over to the hotel. As he suspected, Joyce Sonnerman was waiting in the lobby. He sat down next to her. She smiled faintly. "Quarter to ten, Ben. You don't have much time left."

"I don't need much," Ben said.

"That a fact?"

He smiled. "Yep. Enid doesn't want this wedding any more than I do." He left his chair. "You stick around, Joyce."

She jumped up when he started to leave and grabbed his arm. "Ben, take the money and get out."

"Uhn-uh," he said, and walked out.

Standing on the porch, Ben saw that the Wyatts were still in town; Wyatt's new buggy was parked farther down the street. And Ringo was still hanging around.

Ten o'clock came and with it Anse Sonnerman and Enid. Sonnerman had three men with him, and, as they wheeled by, the old man gave Ben Dembrow a steady stare. Enid rode with her eyes downcast, and Ben hated the old man for making her like that.

Sheriff Arly Burke came down the street, saw

Ben on the hotel porch, and crossed over. He blew out a cloudy breath and studied it. "I think it's getting a shade warmer," he said. "Could bring on more snow."

"To hell with the snow," Ben said quietly.

Burke glanced at him. "Looks like the patriarch and his clan have gathered for the nuptials. Figured out what to do?"

"Yep."

Burke shrugged. "Well, good luck then." He stepped off down the street, then turned around and came back. "Ben, you did leave your gun at home, didn't you?"

"Yeah, sure," Ben said.

This seemed to relieve Arly Burke's mind for he smiled and went on about his business.

An hour can drag, and this one did for Ben Dembrow. He waited on the hotel porch until the last minute, then walked around the block to the preacher's house on a back street. Anse Sonnerman's buggy was tied up in front. Ben walked slowly toward the porch.

One of Sonnerman's hands answered the door. "In the parlor," he said. Ben walked down the hall, then stopped in the archway. The preacher looked uncomfortable, his fingers continually flicking the pages of his Bible. Anse Sonnerman stood rifle-barrel straight in his stiff collar and good suit. Enid remained by his side, held there by his grip on her arm.

Sonnerman turned slowly, looked at Ben, then said: "Your place is by her."

"Er . . . can't we have a little music?" the preacher asked. "My wife plays the organ well."

"Never mind the music," Sonnerman said flatly. "Just read the words over these two."

The front door opened and Joyce came in. She said nothing, just stood to one side and waited. Ben moved over to where Enid stood.

She lifted her face to him. "This is a horrible dream, Ben. I'm sorry."

"Er . . . are we ready?" The preacher's nervousness was increasing.

"We've been ready," Anse Sonnerman snapped. "Get on with it."

The preacher cleared his throat, then spent a maddening moment trying to find the service in his book. Anse Sonnerman kept running a finger under a too-tight collar. Ben could hear everyone breathe, so quiet was it in the parsonage. The preacher had a high, rasping voice, and he faltered considerably, but the wedding ceremony was much shorter than Ben Dembrow had imagined.

Ben suddenly woke up to the fact that the preacher was saying: "Now you may kiss the bride, young man."

Anse Sonnerman made the decision there, too. "No time for that prattle, sir." He looked squarely at Ben. "I won't say I'm welcoming you to the family, Dembrow, but since you'll be moving in under my roof, you'll do as I say. My boys will tear down your fence, and I'll give you a fair price for your place, seein' as how you've put a heap of work into it. Now you take your bride and get on out to my place. . . ."

"Shut up," said Ben mildly.

Anse Sonnerman's eyes widened and he took a step backward before he caught himself. "What was that you said?"

"I said shut up. Now get this through your bony head. I'm not moving in under your roof. Enid doesn't want this crazy marriage. I respect her for a fine girl . . . so you take her home with you." Ben wheeled on his heel, and stalked out.

He went directly to the saloon, banging the door hard enough to make the bartender frown. A few men sitting at the tables looked up, then went back to their cards or talk. "Let me have a bottle," Ben said.

The bartender shook his head. "Your money's no good here. Sorry."

"Who the hell said anything about paying for it? Charge it."

"Now you know I can't do . . ."

Ben Dembrow placed his hands flat on the bar. "If I have to come around and take what I want, a few bottles are liable to get busted."

"Now, Ben, you don't want trouble."

"Man, I got more than you ever saw. Now how about that drink?"

245

"Sure, Ben. Sure." The bartender poured.

Ben tossed it off, then stood there with watery eyes and a solid flame reaching to his stomach.

Arly Burke came in and stepped up to the bar. He looked at Ben Dembrow, then helped himself to the bottle. "You did the right thing, Ben."

Ben Dembrow said nothing.

Burke went on softly: "Right-thinking people will know there was nothing between the girl and you." He rotated his whiskey glass, leaving small circles of dampness on the bar top. "And if you'd taken her home or went to his place, you'd have been through as a rancher. Sonnerman would have gobbled you up."

"Enid didn't want the marriage, either."

"Sure," Burke said. "But you got a new problem." He nodded toward the street. "Dan Ringo's out there. Wants to talk to you."

"Huh? What about?"

"Seems he's lost face in Rimrock," Burke said evenly. "Figures that you're the only one that can give it back."

"He got a gun?"

The sheriff nodded.

Ben paused for a moment. "I better go talk to him."

"Without a gun?"

Ben Dembrow rubbed his hands against the legs of his pants. "I don't reckon he'll shoot me unarmed." He stepped toward the door, hesitated, then walked out onto the porch. People stood along the street, for Dan Ringo's presence was like a shout, calling them. The Sonnermans, old man and daughters, were in front of the hotel, waiting in their buggy. Farther down, Dave Wyatt sat in his new buggy, derby cocked to one side, cigar fragrantly ignited.

Dan Ringo faced the saloon, coatless, patient, and cold sober.

Ben stopped on the porch edge. "You want to see me, Dan?"

Ringo's face tipped back slightly and a brightness came into his eyes. "This is the day, Ben. The day to settle up once and for all."

"I'm not carrying a gun," Ben said. "Do we have to shoot over this?"

"No other way. Burke won't interfere. This is between you and me."

"I see no reason for this," Ben said.

"Ain't what *you* want. I'm calling this tune, Ben. Better get yourself a gun and come back out. If you don't, I'll have to come in after you." He pulled out his watch and glanced at it. "Ten minutes ought to be time enough."

The talk was over; Ben knew it, and went back inside the saloon. Sheriff Arly Burke was still leaning on the bar and Ben sided him. Ben said softly: "The damn' fool!"

"If he draws first and wins," Burke said, "I'll arrest him."

Ben Dembrow snorted.

Burke remained silent for a time. "You handle a gun all right, Ben?"

Ben shrugged. He glanced at the wall clock. Seven minutes left. How could three minutes go by so fast?

Reaching under his coat, Arly Burke unbuckled his gun belt and laid it on the bar. "That trigger is tied back with rawhide, so if you don't know how to slip-hammer shoot, don't pick it up."

Ben Dembrow looked at the gun, then said: "I've done some."

Five minutes left by the wall clock.

Ben shed his Mackinaw, laying it on the bar. He scooped up Arly Burke's rig and buckled it around his waist, settling the holster on his hip. Then he bent to knot the tie-down around his thigh.

Arly Burke watched thoughtfully.

The gentlemen at the table got up together and followed Ben to the door. When he stepped outside, they quickly moved along the porch, where they had a good view and yet were removed from the possibility of catching any stray lead. The sheriff came out also and took a station ten yards down, his face smoothly unreadable.

Dan Ringo straightened when he saw Ben wearing a gun. Then Ringo advanced to the exact center of the snow-covered street.

Ben walked to the edge of the porch and stood there, looking down-tilted at Ringo, saying: "If this is the way it's got to be . . . then let's have it."

A silent minute paraded by, broken only by the restless stamping of a horse and some snow sliding off the harness maker's roof. Ringo stood rock still, then his hand whipped toward his gun. He had the edge on Ben Dembrow; his gun cleared first and started to come up, but he was on the street level and had to raise it an extra bit while Ben had only half the distance to cover in the same split second.

Ben let his thumb slip off the polished hammer at just the right instant, and Ringo's shot blended a hair tardy, the bullet scarring the porch planks by Ben's feet. Ben's bullet caught Ringo high in the chest, flinging him completely around. Ringo struck the street solidly on his back, then arched it in agony before sagging limply. Blood began to make a pink bed for him.

Ben unbuckled the gun belt, handing it to Arly Burke when he came up.

Burke said something, but Ben didn't seem to hear. Ben stepped off the porch and walked over to where Ringo lay. The crowd started to move in, then stopped as Ben bent over the dead man.

Burke was with him, asking: "What's the matter, Ben?"

"He turned down a fight yesterday," Ben said flatly. He tried not to look into Dan Ringo's sightless eyes. His hands were flipping around Ringo's pockets. "Funny he'd suddenly get proddy."

Then he patted a pocket and looked quickly at Burke before pulling out a packet of banknotes.

"What the hell?" Burke said.

Ben stood up, his glance whipping to the Sonnermans, who still sat in their buggy in front of the hotel. His stride was long as he paced across the street. Anse Sonnerman's expression was bland but there was caution in his eyes as Ben Dembrow stopped near the off wheel, the money in his hands.

Then suddenly Ben flung the banknotes in Sonnerman's face. "Here's your money back, old man. He didn't do as good a job as you thought he would, did he?"

Sonnerman tipped his head forward and looked at the banknotes in his lap. His eyes were genuinely puzzled. "Dembrow, I don't know what you're talking about."

"You're a liar!"

Spots of brightness appeared in the old man's cheeks. "Now, see . . ."

The look in Ben Dembrow's eyes cut him short. "How low can you get, old man? Hiring another man to kill me." He swung away, but Arly Burke had come up and now he caught Ben's arm.

"Hold on a minute. How do you know about that money, Ben?"

"Joyce Sonnerman offered it to me. I told you, Sheriff. Now that she found out she couldn't buy me, she gave it to Ringo to kill me."

"That's not true!" Joyce said loudly. She looked at her father. "All right, I did try to buy him off with the money. I didn't want you to know about it, that's all."

Anse Sonnerman's shame was a banner on his face. Slowly he got down from the buggy and faced Arly Burke. "I expect you'll want to hold me until you investigate this?"

"Yes," Burke said. "If you'll wait in my office. . . ."

"Of course," Sonnerman said, and walked down the street with weary steps.

Ben looked at Enid, sitting stiffly and ready to cry any minute. She said: "How you must hate us, Ben. How terrible you must think we are."

"I'm sorry to have hurt you," he said, and turned away, no longer able to look at her, sitting there, so helpless and lonely.

VI

At the livery stable, Ben Dembrow saddled his horse and rode out of town, hoping to leave behind all the concentrated unpleasantness he had found there. He could not get the picture of Dan Ringo dead on the snow out of his mind.

Before he reached the home place, the wind completed its swing, backing off to the northeast and settling down to a steady blow. The sky was muddying up with weather and he judged that it ought to be on them by morning. More snow, probably, and a sudden drop in temperature afterward to make life tough.

He stabled his horse as soon as he got home, then built a fire in the stove and cooked a pot of coffee. While he was drinking it, he heard a team wheel into the yard. He stepped to the door, and saw Dave Wyatt and Elizabeth dismount.

Wyatt was in a jubilant mood. He came in, blowing on his hands and smiling. Elizabeth gave Ben a tired smile, a pat on the arm, then helped herself to the coffee.

"Burke locked Sonnerman in jail," Wyatt said, plopping down in a chair. He brought out one of his cigars and lighted it carefully. "The old bear's been treed, Ben, and you done it, boy. You done it. You got him licked! I'll pass the word around among the farmers in the Yellows and they'll back you to the man."

"Kind of a different tune you're singing now, ain't it?"

"A smart man always chooses the winner," Dave Wyatt said. "Was a time this morning when I thought you was done for, but you faced Ringo, and that weather-cocked everything the other way. Sonnerman will have a hell of a time explainin' that to the law, believe you me. . . . Elizabeth, fix your old dad a cup of coffee." Then Wyatt looked back at Ben Dembrow. "Sonnerman's cattle are crowdin' your fence. And there's more weather making. A lot of 'em are goin' to freeze to death on their feet. Costs money to lose cattle that way." He chuckled. "By the time Sonnerman gets out of jail, he's liable to find himself broke, ain't he?"

"You think that's funny?" asked Ben.

Dave Wyatt sobered immediately. "Not funny, Ben, but damned necessary. With him against the wall, we can move out of the damned mountain valleys onto some good land."

"You got good land," Ben said.

"A man wants better," Dave Wyatt said, standing up. He looked around the cabin. "Needs cleanin'," he said. "Hate a dirty place. Elizabeth, why don't you stay and clean up for Ben. Woman's work anyway. I'll stop for you on my way to town, or else Ben can bring you home."

"There's no need to do that," Ben said.

"Now, I won't hear different," Wyatt said, going outside "Friends are friends, Ben. And Elizabeth likes doing for you. She surely does."

He was a difficult man to argue with, Ben knew, simply because he kept walking away, instead of standing still to talk it out. Dave Wyatt mounted his new buggy and lifted the reins. His cigar was tilted upward and he patted his derby to seat it squarely. A lift of his hand and he turned out, leaving Ben Dembrow with an open mouth and no one to talk to.

When Ben went back into the cabin, Elizabeth was washing the dishes. She turned as he closed the door. "Do you really mind, Ben?"

"No," he said. "I'm glad for the company."

"I thought I was more than that." She dried her hands and came up to him, her palms against his cheeks. "In town I thought you were going to break down, the way you looked at Enid just before you left."

"Do we have to talk about her?"

"No, not if you don't want to. Look at me." She held his face straight. "What kind of a girl is she, standing there like a whipped pup? I'd fight for you, Ben."

The pressure of her hands pulled his face down until their lips met, then there was no more need for holding him; her lips did that. He put his arms around and held her until she gasped, but she found pleasure in the hurt. There was magnificent passion in her and she told him so with her lips. When he pulled away, his hands shook.

Elizabeth Wyatt smiled and watched him carefully from behind the screen of her long eyelashes. "Can she do that?"

Ben smiled. "You're forgetting that I'm married."

"She'll never be your wife," Elizabeth said, and put her arms around his waist, laying her head against his chest. "You're strong, Ben. The kind of a man every woman wants. You reach out and take what you want because that's the way you are. I want to be taken that way. You're a hard man. Even ruthless."

He said quietly: "All I wanted was a place of my own so I could make a living."

"You're too big to stay small." She moved her hands, phrasing her thoughts in her mind. "You're going to take Anse Sonnerman's place in this valley. And I'm going right along with you, every step of the way. You won't weaken for what you have to do because I won't let you. I'll give you strength. That's more than Enid could ever give you because she has none."

He turned around and looked carefully at her. "What do you want, Elizabeth?"

"You, Ben."

He thought about this for a moment, then said: "I've got stock to tend."

She offered no argument for she was wise enough to let him come around, as she was sure he would. He shrugged into his coat, tied a muffler around his head, and went out. During the rest of the day he hauled feed from the barn to his horse sheds. He watched the weather carefully, gauged the wind often, and tried to get the bearing of the storm that was surely coming.

Darkness was slipping in when he started toward the cabin, now a black shadow except for the shafts of yellow light pouring from the windows to make bright patches on the snow.

The cold air carried sound and he looked around as a rider approached, coming along the corral fence. Ben waited until the rider turned into the yard, and, when he approached, he saw that it was Enid. She had three huge canvas satchels tied onto the saddle and a great coat muffled her to the ears.

"Ben?" she said timidly.

"Hello. I never expected to see you."

"Can I get down?"

He went around and lifted her to the ground. She glanced at him, then pulled her eyes away. "I . . . I wasn't sure that you wanted me, but I had to come. I'm your wife, Ben. I want to be your wife."

That she could swallow her pride and come to him like this left him feeling small and humble. He took her arm. "We'll talk about it inside where it's warm."

He opened the door for her, and they stepped inside quickly to shut out the cold. Enid turned first, her hands raised to shed the scarf she had over her head. And she stood that way as though suddenly frozen.

Ben Dembrow turned around and gasped.

Elizabeth had filled the large wooden tub and

was sitting in it, watching them, water cascading off her smooth shoulders. Almost indolently she reached for a towel and then casually dried her hair. There was a stunned moment of silence, then Enid sobbed and whirled, fighting the latch in her haste to get out.

"Wait," Ben said, and bolted after her.

But she ran toward her horse, stumbling once. When he tried to pick her up, she slapped him fiercely. "Go back to her!" she cried, clawing for the saddle horn. She was crying openly now, and, before Ben Dembrow could stop her, she wheeled and raced out of the yard.

He started to run after her, then realized how foolish that was. Slowly he turned back to the cabin and went inside. Elizabeth was out of the tub, moving about with a towel wrapped around her waist and another over her shoulders. Ben stopped just inside the door and asked: "Why, Elizabeth?"

She shrugged. "You wouldn't have made it plain enough. As luck would have it, I did."

He shook his head. "You're a bitter girl. It changes you."

She thought about that, and sighed deeply. She turned her back, unwrapped one towel, then slipped into her shift. Once she glanced at Ben Dembrow and said: "What are you going to do?"

"When you get dressed, I'm going to take you home."

She thought this over, too, then murmured: "I must be getting old." When she got into her dress, she backed up to him so he could lace it. "Ben, I never give up. You ought to know that." She canted her head to one side and gave him a quick kiss.

He reacted like a wooden image and she pouted. "I wish you'd stop thinking about her," she said.

"Almost did," he admitted. "But you couldn't be satisfied with half the victory." He stepped over to the bed and picked up her coat, handing it to her. She could have argued, but didn't. When she was bundled up, he opened the door and stood there until she went past him.

Rather than leave a horse or lead one back, Ben boosted her into the saddle and rode double, cutting immediately toward the pass road. The wind had picked up in tempo and there was no talk because of it; neither seemed to be in the mood for conversation. Ben had picked a paint gelding with a lot of stamina and he topped the pass thirty minutes later, cutting off on the narrow road leading to Dave Wyatt's place.

When he rode into the yard, Elizabeth slid off. "Come in, Ben. I don't want there to be any bad thoughts between us."

"Not now," he said. "Good night, Elizabeth."

"Wait," she said, and fastened her hands into his coat. She pulled him low and tipped her head back for his kiss. She was a woman who wanted much, but had a great deal to give in return and her lips reminded him of this. Finally she released him and hurried toward the door. He waited until she went inside, then started home again.

Before he hit the pass road the snow began, not a lazy, drifting snow but a driving fury that blocked out all vision and stung his face like countless needles. The shocking suddenness with which the storm descended made him think of Enid. She couldn't be more than a third of the way home and with this swirling down across the flats, she could get lost and freeze to death before anyone found her.

The thought of her dying drove Ben Dembrow to kick his horse into a senseless run, ignoring the attending dangers. With numbing clarity he realized now how he could look on Elizabeth Wyatt with the lamplight making satin of her flesh and not feel a desire for her. There was only one woman who he desired, and now she would be fighting blindly in a swooping, sight-smothering blanket.

Ben was forced to slow down; the risk of a fatal fall was great. Yet he went on as fast as he could and by instinct reached his own yard. He dismounted and ran into the house for the blankets off his bed and, with these in hand, started out along his corral fence in the direction Enid would have to take. Tracking her was out of the question for the wind had wiped the land to a clean white plain.

His horses were nosed in their shelters, while on the other side of the fence Anse Sonnerman's cattle were fully exposed to the storm's driving fury. They bawled and lunged, trying to get through to the shelter higher on, shelter they knew was there and needed for survival.

A sudden thought struck him startlingly clear. He still owed Anse Sonnerman considerable money. He could now discharge that debt.

Ben went to work with wire clippers. Then he sat his horse and watched everything sweep to the sheltered pockets in the pass, horses and cattle alike. The mass of cattle would keep his horses from straying through the cut fence. Besides that, this was one night animals would not be likely to stray from shelter.

Once again he faced head-on into the tearing strength of the storm. Visibility was almost nothing and he was startled immeasurably when he drove his horse head first into another.

Enid screamed in fright. Ben jumped to the ground, running to her, grabbing for the bridle of her frightened mount.

"You're all right," he kept saying. "You're all right. You're safe now."

He led her horse after mounting his own. As they passed his cut fence line, Enid cried: "Oh, Ben!"

He went on, rounding at last the cabin corner that afforded shelter from the wind. They could catch their breath there and he lifted her from her horse.

"I tried to find the herd," she said quickly. "But they were gone, Ben. I was following the track . . . when you bumped into me."

"It's all right," he told her. "Get into the house."

She stopped. "Not with her there, Ben."

"She's not there. Go on in. I'll put up the horses." He opened the door and pushed her inside, then went to the barn and turned the horses into a stall. Her satchels were still tied to her saddle. He carried them to the cabin.

She was standing before the fire, toasting the chill from her. The tub of water was still sitting there and Enid looked at it, then at Ben as he closed the door and set her satchels down.

"I'll get that out of here," Ben said, starting toward the tub.

"No! Leave it," Enid said. "I'm the intruder here."

"You're not," Ben said. "How can I explain it, when it looks so bad?"

Her glance came around, level and direct. "Tell me the truth, Ben."

"I never touched her," Ben said. He watched her for a heartbeat, then Enid put her hands over her face and cried. Timidly he put his hand on her shoulder and, when she did not resist, slid his arms around her. "I love you, Enid. Funny I never knew it until the storm hit and I thought you were lost in it. You belong here. No one else could ever take your place."

He found that he could kiss her, and he learned that a fire in a woman could be a consuming thing of magnificent splendor. Then he held her close to him, not speaking.

Finally she said: "You cut the fence. Why did you do it?"

"Saving the cattle for your father wiped out my debt to him. We're more than even now."

He went outside for more firewood, and to take a look at the storm. There was no increase in the wind and the snow came down as furiously as ever. When he went back inside, he saw that she was unpacking her satchels. Expecting clothes, he was surprised to find that she had made curtains, and a cloth for the table, which fit perfectly.

She smiled shyly. "I used to come here and mentally measure everything, Ben. Then I'd go home and make the things and put them away. When Father made us get married, I wanted to tell you so badly that it was what I really wanted. But I didn't know how. I just didn't know."

"And I hurt you," he said.

"Not really. When you love someone, you can understand a lot. And you never knew how I really felt about you." She stopped talking, turning her head quickly toward the door. "Did you hear someone call?"

"No," he said.

"Wait! There it is again."

Ben Dembrow started for the door, but, before he got there, it burst open and Dave Wyatt stood, spraddle-legged, his face wildly angry. He slammed the door with his foot, gave Enid a black look, then faced Ben.

"Idiot!" he shouted. "You went and cut the fence." He was so upset that he shook. "You had Sonnerman bent over backward and you let him go! Oh, you fool!"

"Set down and cool off," Ben said. "What I do is my business, and you better remember that I didn't get any help from you."

"Ha! Little you know! Why, I stood behind you every step of the way, fixin' it so you couldn't back down. You think I wanted to see that old hog in the valley? I got a right to my share, you hear?"

"You don't make sense," Ben said softly, hoping to calm Dave Wyatt by example. "Sit down, and have some coffee. You must be froze stiff."

"I'm fine," Wyatt declared. "Better than you're going to be because I might still come out on top." He looked at Enid. "Too bad you're here. Wish you wasn't, but that don't matter now." His glance whipped back to Ben Dembrow. "You've been bustin' a gut wondering, so I'll tell you. I took your money. Elizabeth slipped it out of your pocket when she was in the yard with you." He laughed. "Without that money you had to fight Sonnerman. Always smart to get another man to do your fightin'. That way a man's sure of bein' alive to pick up the winnings."

Ben Dembrow felt a cool wind of caution blow through him. He backed up to the table and leaned there, hands spread. "Pretty smart of you, Dave. I was never sure, you know." He nodded, then added: "I guess I don't have to wonder any more where Dan Ringo got the five hundred dollars."

"Bet your boots you don't," Wyatt said. "Hell, you think I could take a chance on your not goin' along with Sonnerman?" He looked at Enid and smiled. "You ain't put together like my Elizabeth, but I reckon you could be fun enough once you got started."

Ben Dembrow saw color creep into Enid's face and slid his voice neatly into the lull. "But you've lost. I whipped your scheme when I cut that fence and let the cattle through."

"Thought that myself," Wyatt said flatly. "Thought it all the way down here, but now I've changed my mind." He cocked his head toward the storm outside. "Freeze pretty quick out there, couldn't you?" His glance came around to Enid. "She'd freeze quicker, 'specially if she didn't have any clothes on."

Ben caught his breath and hardly dared to ask. "What are you talking about, Dave?"

"Her," Wyatt said. "I'll shoot you, then rip her garments a bit and shove her out. Won't be hard to drive her a mile or so. When the storm blows over, I'll take you to Sonnerman. Make a pretty convincin' story, how she come to you for help and how you insisted on your legal rights. Who'll doubt it? Especially after the way you acted in town after killin' Ringo? Arly Burke'll believe it. He'll have to. Sonnerman ought to be properly grateful to me for killing his daughter's murderer. Likely I'll move down into the valley, after all." He scratched his face. " 'Course, it might be spring before the snow melts enough for Sonnerman to find her, but you'll be dead, so you won't care."

"Dave, you're crazy!"

"Yep," he admitted. "Like a fox. Ben, you don't understand me. Worked my last poor section of land. I deserve better and I'm going to have my due. All my life I've been pushed by the big men. My turn now to be big."

Wyatt dipped a hand into his coat pocket and Ben didn't have to guess what was going to come out. Reaching behind him, he scooped up the glass-base lamp and threw it as Dave Wyatt shot right through the pocket. Ben felt the bullet hit his arm, and then the lamp caught Wyatt flush in the chest, shattering the chimney and spilling flame and coal oil over his fur coat.

Wyatt shot again and missed, then the coat was on fire and he was beating at the flames with both hands, screaming at the top of his lungs. He whirled toward the door, flung it open, then went charging out across the snow, falling, rolling, trying to put out the fire. Ben made the door in two jumps and would have gone after him had not Enid held him fast.

The storm took second place to Wyatt's yelling, and through the swirl of snow the ball of fire thrashed about wildly, without direction. Enid closed her eyes tightly and clapped both hands over her ears. Ben reached for his coat, intending to start after Wyatt, but he realized how hopeless pursuit was. The man was running with insane speed, now out of sight in the driving storm. In another minute he would be hopelessly lost.

Ben closed the door and leaned against it, aware then that a trickle of blood was oozing down his arm. Enid saw the drops form on his finger tips and ran for a towel while Ben stripped off his shirt and undershirt. The bullet had caught him squarely, but the fur of Wyatt's coat had slowed the low-powered .41 Derringer to the point where it did little more than break the skin. Ben could pick the bullet out with his fingers.

She washed the wound carefully and bandaged it. Afterward Ben sat humped over in the chair, staring at the fire. "Wyatt wanted too much, Enid."

Enid nodded, saying softly: "I feel sorry for the girl."

"Don't. She can take care of herself, better than you think." He sighed deeply. "Storm will let up by morning. I'll get outside there and figure some way to keep my horses from straying off. I won't have to sell my horses now."

She knelt by him and rested her head on his knee. "Ben, we're going to do fine here."

He bent down and kissed her with great gentleness.

She was immensely happy. She got up and moved about the cabin, stopping by the bed. "This is very soft. Feathers?"

"Wild duck," he admitted.

Enid smiled demurely. "Ben . . . you might draw a fresh tub of water for me."

He lugged the tub to the door, then outside where he dumped it to one side so it wouldn't freeze into a dangerous ice slick. At the well he dropped the heavy wooden bucket a few times to break the ice, then carried water inside and filled several large kettles on the stove.

He checked the barn door for lack of something else to do, and after ten minutes went back toward the cabin. At the door, he laughed at the howling fury of the storm—then he went inside.

ABOUT THE AUTHOR

Will Cook is the author of numerous outstanding Western novels as well as historical frontier fiction. He was born in Richmond, Indiana, but was raised by an aunt and uncle in Cambridge, Illinois. He joined the U.S. Cavalry at the age of sixteen but was disillusioned because horses were being eliminated through mechanization. He transferred to the U.S. Army Air Force in which he served in the South Pacific during the Second World War. Cook turned to writing in 1951 and contributed a number of outstanding short stories to *Dime Western* and other pulp magazines as well as fiction for major smooth-paper magazines such as *The Saturday Evening Post*. Sometimes in his short stories Cook would introduce characters that would later be featured in novels, such as Charlie Boomhauer who first appeared in "Lawmen Die Sudden" in *Big-Book Western* in 1953 and is later to be found in *Badman's Holiday* (1958) and *The Wind River Kid* (1958). Along with his steady productivity, Cook maintained an enviable quality. His novels range widely in time and place, from the Illinois frontier of 1811 to southwest Texas in 1905, but each is peopled with credible and interesting characters whose interactions form the backbone of the narrative. Indeed, his fiction is known for its strong heroines. Another common feature is Cook's compassion for his characters that must be able to survive in a wild and violent land. His protagonists make mistakes, hurt people they care for, and sometimes succumb to ignoble impulses, but this all provides an added dimension to the artistry of his work.

ABOUT THE EDITOR

Bill Pronzini was born in Petaluma, California. His earliest Western fiction was published under his own name and a variety of pseudonyms in *Zane Grey Western Magazine.* Among his most notable Western novels are *Starvation Camp* (1984) and *Firewind* (1989). He is also the editor of numerous Western story collections, including *Under the Burning Sun: Western Stories* (Five Star Westerns, 1997) by H.A. DeRosso, *Renegade River: Western Stories* (Five Star Westerns, 1998) by Giff Cheshire, and *Tracks in the Sand* by H.A. DeRosso (2001), among others. His Western story collection, *All the Long Years* (Five Star Westerns, 2001), was followed by *Burgade's Crossing* (Five Star Westerns, 2003) and *Quincannon's Game* (Five Star Westerns, 2005).

Additional Copyright Information:

Center Point Large Print
600 Brooks Road / PO Box 1
Thorndike, ME 04986-0001 USA

(207) 568-3717

US & Canada:
1 800 929-9108
www.centerpointlargeprint.com